A NIKKI PAGE MYSTERY
BOOK 4

Continued on Page Four

SHERYL STEINES

NIKKI PAGE MYSTERIES

New Page
Back Page
Page Three Girls
Continued on Page Four

A coming of middle age story

CONTINUED ON PAGE FOUR

ISBN 13: 979-8-9906194-5-6

Cover by Mallory Rock, Rock Solid Book Designs

Edited by Stephanie Elmore

CHAPTER 1

"This is Nikki Page," I said as I answered a call from an unknown number.

An unfamiliar voice introduced herself. "I'm Mrs. McDaniels, Mrs. Page. We've sent you several e-mails that you've seemingly ignored," she said in an exasperated voice.

"I haven't ignored them. Exactly. I've been busy," I said as I searched through my huge pile of papers looking for the instruction booklet.

"We really need you to send in your work hours for the state licensing department otherwise you won't get credit, and you'll lose your temporary license and have to start over." She was only doing her job as a career specialist with the private investigator program I was currently neck deep in, as I prepared for the licensure test.

But it had been a busy week. I let out a sigh as I searched the pile of papers, looking for my instruction booklet.

"I know. I thought I had another week to turn it in. Is there a reason you're calling me about it, now?" I asked as I stared at the form, specifically the blank field for PI name. I was required to find myself an established PI in which to obtain my training hours. I hadn't yet, there had been too much going on.

When wasn't there?

"We're reminding all of our students who have not sent us the PI they'll be working with. We need that name now."

I only knew one PI, but I hadn't called him yet.

"Okay. I thought I had one more week. I'll call him today and get it set up," I said, as I tried to keep my voice calm.

"That's fine, Mrs. Page. As long as I get it by tomorrow, you'll be admitted to take the test."

"Thank you. I'm so very sorry," I finally said as I stared at the empty form. But Mrs. McDaniels had already hung up.

I had been busy, between studying for the PI test and my job with attorney Samuel Ross. While the job was no longer full time since the death of his partner and my one-time kidnapper and almost murderer, there was still much to do to close up his law firm. It hadn't helped that Will's ex-wife had been murdered shortly after. Frankly, with everything going on, I forgot to call the PI.

I sighed again. Things had been going so well for all of us over the last few weeks and yet, I was convinced the other shoe would fall and then it had. Everything changed one week ago, when Will called me to tell me he found his ex-wife, Janelle Mann, murdered in her home.

It had been a stressful three hours for Will as he answered question after question, as the police pulled me in to answer more questions. The night after Janelle was killed, I finally arrived home and had fallen into bed late that night, unable to process what had happened. Between the time of death, Will's alibi and the fact he had no gunshot residue on his hands or suit, the police eventually determined he was innocent of Janelle's murder.

In the week since, he had been questioned again while at work and again at the house, mostly filling in blanks about Janelle's life where he could. It had been a week since her death, and we thought we were through with the investigation.

But in the aftermath of her murder, Janelle's death still hurt. She was once a friend and Will had been with her for twenty years. We both needed to mourn in our own ways.

It would take some time.

But life didn't stop. Things still needed to be done.

I pulled myself back to my present situation and stared at the form I needed to complete by tomorrow. That meant I needed to call a PI.

I could use someone from the book the school provided, but I wanted to work with someone I knew, so I called the only PI I knew.

I dialed Stan Marley.

He was affable, and helpful when I called him regarding a twenty-year-old missing person's case I worked on when I was working for Will in his family law practice. I hoped he'd remember me as I dialed his number. I didn't push send.

The man was in his seventies, and our interaction during the case had been brief, but then…

I pushed send and waited. Three rings… four rings… a voice mail.

"Hi, Stan. This is Nikki Page. I don't know if you remember me. You helped me find Sabrina and Melanie Crew. Well, I'm hoping you might be able to help me again. I'm studying… well I started studying for the PI licensure test. I need a PI for an apprenticeship. I was wondering… Oh, this is stupid," I muttered.

"Hello, Mrs. Page?"

I recognized his gravelly voice as he picked up his phone.

"Yes. It's Nikki Page. How are you, Mr. Marley?"

"Well not as good as you it sounds like. The PI exam. If I remember correctly, you found Sabrina and Melanie when I couldn't. And you solved a cold case murder. Wanna investigate for a living now, huh?"

I felt my cheeks flush. Of course he remembers. Of course I'm an idiot. I wiped my sweaty palms on my jean shorts.

"Yeah. It seemed like a good combination as a paralegal. The last bit, I need a PI to oversee the apprenticeship. I thought of you." I smiled awkwardly as I said that. Thankfully, he couldn't see me.

"Hmmm," he said. "I suppose I can help you. Since you know more than the average apprentice, just starting out, I think I can take on an apprentice. What do you need from me?"

"For now, I need a form completed with your name and contact info and my schedule so the hours can be tracked. Can I send you the form?"

"Send it to my email. I'll get it back to you today. You still with Will Mann's firm?"

"No. It was only temporary. I'm working for a lawyer named Samuel Ross as he closes his office. He just lost his partner," I said. It was so much more than that considering Ethan Grater had killed his partner in an entertainment company, and he tried to kill me when I discovered what he had done. The least I could do was stay on to help Samuel retire.

"Samuel Ross? That was you Ethan Grater tried to kill? I heard about that."

"It was me."

"Damn, Nikki. You really know how to get at 'em, don't you?"

I chuckled. "I do my best, apparently."

"You realize there're a lot of hours you need to put in. When's your licensing exam?"

"September. I need this info by tomorrow so we can get everything set up in the program system and make sure I get all the hours."

"Okay. Send me the form. I'll fill it out. How long are you with Samuel Ross?"

"Another three weeks should have the office cleaned out and the files moved to where they need to go."

"Good. Great. Call me when you're done, and I'll have you come in. I'm looking forward to this."

"So am I. And thank you."

Since I finally had this working, I sent a digital copy of the form to Stan Marley, pleased with myself for finally making the call.

I cleaned up the large pile of documents and mail I still needed to review and determine if I was going to toss, shred, or save.

Advertising went directly into the garbage can, opened

envelopes sorted by subject, took out letters for Emily and Jacob and placed them in another pile.

There was a hand addressed letter to me, no return address, and post marked eight days ago.

I stared at the unopened letter, began to open it when my phone rang. I glanced at the screen.

"Shit," I said. "This is Nikki."

"Hi, Nikki. It's Barry Mintz." Why was Will's lawyer calling me?

"Hi, Barry. Now what's happened?" Whatever it was, I knew it wouldn't be good.

"The police arrested Will."

"What? Why?" I nearly shouted it. He had cooperated fully. Answered their questions, they even admitted he wasn't responsible. He had an alibi!

"They found something in Janelle's house that goes to motive. Can you come to the Palatine Police Station?"

"What about his alibi? The negative gunshot residue test? The missing murder weapon? What could they possibly have found?"

"Nikki, it's bullshit, and the police know it."

But it wasn't bullshit if they arrested Will. "I'll be there in thirty minutes," I said.

My piles would have to wait. Absently, I shoved the mystery letter in my purse and headed to my car. After fumbling with the keys, I turned over the engine. I took a minute to breathe before backing out and heading to the police station.

***

I raced to the first open parking spot in the small, suburban police parking lot. My hands trembled as I shut down the car. Sweat dripped from my neck, down my back. I took several breaths in an attempt to calm myself. One glance in the mirror, I could see the stress as much as I could feel it. Using a tissue, I patted away the moisture, tossed the tissue, and grabbed my purse. I ran for the entrance and shuddered in the cold lobby as I searched for a receptionist.

She glanced up as I walked over; her look, if I had to guess, conveyed annoyance. Maybe it was the crinkled eyes or the pursed lips. Either way my presence felt unwelcome. I didn't care.

"Will Mann. Where is he?" I asked briskly.

"I'm sorry, but you can't go back there."

Before I could argue, Barry Mintz appeared from the interrogation room. "She's with me," he said gently. The receptionist, as I now noticed, was named Susan, nodded but wasn't happy she had to let me go.

"I need to see her identification."

I rolled my eyes but didn't protest as I rooted around in my purse. I saw the anonymous letter, as I found my wallet and plucked out my driver's license, finally handing it to her.

She glanced at it and back to me. I had never felt so awkward with sweat on my neck, my face glistening, and my hair a frizzy mess.

Susan searched her desk and handed me both my ID and a visitor's pass I quickly attached to my shirt. I followed Barry to the viewing room.

"What did they find?" I asked as Barry closed the door behind us.

He held his hand up as if to force me to calm or maybe for him to gather himself. It didn't help me. I was quivering so badly; I could barely stand, and I nearly fell into the metal chair when I sat.

"They think they found motive. But they haven't clued me in yet."

"That's…" I couldn't believe this was happening. To me, to Will, to us. Arresting the wrong person wouldn't help Janelle now. "He didn't do this. He has an alibi," I said.

"The police want to talk to you. I'll represent you if that works for you. At least for this. Tell them the truth and only answer the questions they ask."

"I know," I snapped as I looked through the viewing window where Will sat. He was rubbing his hands against his pant legs.

Barry watched as well. “I need to get back in there. And then I’ll join you again.” He left me alone, and I watched him re-enter the interrogation room and sit beside Will.

Will. I couldn’t imagine what evidence they had found that would give them motive for Janelle’s murder. If it were new evidence, what was it? I wracked my brain, but I couldn’t think of what they had that could explain why Will would have killed Janelle.

I felt like life was moving in slow motion as I watched it unfold in front of me, and I had no control over what was happening.

Beyond the viewing window, Barry whispered to Will. I glanced around for the speaker box and turned it on as I watched.

Barry turned to the viewing window. He couldn’t see me, but our eyes met.

How did we get here again? I thought we were done. Apparently not.

The police detective entered the room and sat across from Will. He put his notebook on the table in front of him, took out his pen and turned on the recording device.

“Benson Clyde, interviewing Will Mann, present, his lawyer Barry Mintz.” The detective looked at Will. “Tell me again, Mr. Mann, when did you get to Janelle’s home the morning, she was found dead?”

Will sighed, put his hands on the table in front of him. "I was badged into the courthouse at eight. By the time I filed the restraining order against Janelle, on Nikki's behalf, it was after ten. I left the courthouse and got to Janelle's at eleven."

Benson Clyde reviewed his notes before looking at Will again. His pale blue eyes looked at Will from under shaggy blond hair. Benson was hyper focused on him.

"You went to see your ex-wife. Why would you do that? You divorced her, it was over. Unless you had unfinished business." He pursed his lips together while he waited for an answer.

"I didn't divorce her. She divorced me," Will scowled. Barry touched his arm. Will calmed. The detective was circling back to questions he had already asked. This created stress with the hope that the constant questioning would trip Will into admitting guilt.

"I'll correct that statement. Janelle divorced you. Which then leads to my original question, why did you go see your ex-wife the morning she died?"

Will ran a hand through his short hair as he counted. I knew that's what he was doing because that's what he always did when he was stressed or upset. It was his way of gaining composure before saying or doing something he'd later regret.

"Janelle's parents asked me to speak with her. They knew I was filing the restraining order. So, I did as they asked. I went to see Janelle."

"What were you hoping to accomplish?" Detective Clyde asked.

Will rubbed the stubble on his chin, placed his hands in his lap.

"After everything Janelle and I had gone through in the last eighteen years, I felt I owed her an explanation for the restraining order. I also believed something was going on with her, and I wanted to know what. She wasn't acting like herself." He stopped for a moment to catch his breath and wipe away a tear.

Benson Clyde saw Will and grimaced.

"Were you mad at Janelle when you went to see her?"

"Mad? No. I was upset, but mostly I was worried."

Clyde made a note in his notebook. "Why were you worried? She wasn't your problem anymore."

"Even though Janelle's behavior was potentially harmful to herself and others, I still cared about what happened to her. She was a smart, beautiful, funny woman. But three years ago, something changed. I don't know what it was, she never said. Instead, she asked for a divorce, and I didn't fight it. When Janelle begged me to come see her, and her parents asked me to talk to her, I went over."

Benson Clyde made a note in his book. "Did she tell you what she wanted to talk about?"

"No. Just that she had something she needed to talk to me about."

"And you just went? After filing a restraining order against your ex-wife. You were afraid she would harm your fiancée and her children. That doesn't sound like someone who still cared about his ex-wife," Benson Clyde said pointedly.

"I still cared," Will murmured.

"Or maybe you went to file the restraining order to give yourself an alibi because murdering Janelle would remove the problem from your life."

Will balled his hands into tight fists.

"I didn't kill her."

"Why did you go to see your ex-wife?" Benson Clyde asked with a raised voice.

"To find out why she was acting the way she was and to explain the restraining order." Will sounded tired, and I feared a little defeated.

Benson Clyde tapped his pencil on his notepad as if thinking of his next question or extending Will's stress.

As I watched, I paced. My mind raced with thoughts of Janelle. We had been friends once, and from what Will had told me, her behavior was indeed unusual, and I had the opportunity to see it firsthand.

Will explained to the police that Janelle's behavior began to change three years ago and yet he was unable to tell them and me for that matter, what had changed for her. I couldn't help but wonder what life-changing event had such an impact that it altered her personality, and yet her husband didn't know about it. I stopped pacing and turned my attention to the interview room.

"Janelle was killed at 8 a.m. Where were you?" Detective Clyde asked.

Will sighed. "I was at the courthouse in Waukegan. I was badged in. They have me on video," Will said, his voice was laced with sarcasm and anger. Mostly, he was pissed by the repeated questions he had already answered days ago.

I couldn't understand why he was still sitting there. He had an alibi. What the hell was going on? I kept thinking of that as I watched Detective Clyde pull something out of the case file: a thin pile of papers.

"We found this in Janelle's home office," the detective said.

Will looked at the blank pages and pulled the pile toward him. "It's my old letterhead. You said you found it at Janelle's?"

Will looked at Barry.

Detective Clyde pulled out another pile of pages. "Don't act surprised, Mr. Mann. You wrote these." He slid the second pile to Will. Will shuffled through what looked like letters, quickly skimming each one. There had to be about ten of them.

Will whispered to his lawyer. I wish I could have heard what he was saying.

"My client doesn't know where these letters came from. He never wrote or signed them. Where did you find these?" Barry asked.

My heart sped up. Will had signed a legal letter for me several weeks ago when I helped a friend out of a situation. I wrote the letter but needed his signature.

Could he have done the same for Janelle?

"They were found in Janelle's files in her home office. If you didn't sign these, where did they come from?"

Will sat straighter as he perused the documents. "These are letters to insurance companies on behalf of Janelle's employer. She worked for Murphy Speech Center. My specialty is family law. I don't practice insurance law. I did not write these letters, and that's not my signature."

While he had done that for me, my request was simply asking a photographer for a signed model release form. This sounded different. Letters to insurance companies regarding patient claims was something else.

But if Janelle had asked, would he have written the letters for her?

"You deny your involvement?" Detective Clyde asked.

"Yes. I deny I wrote these. These are written on my old letterhead. I haven't used this letter head in two years. The letters were written… some eighteen months ago."

My stomach churned at the sight of the letterhead, the signed letters. Even though he had helped me, I couldn't believe he'd take on so many letters for the speech therapy center. They surely had their own law team.

But then, he had done that favor for me.

Detective Clyde pulled the letters and blank letterhead toward his folder and put them inside. "Was she threatening you over your involvement, Mr. Mann? Maybe she was blackmailing you because you had written those letters when, as you say, insurance isn't your expertise. Did she threaten you with the letters? Threaten to expose your involvement in these therapy cases?" The detective stared at Will, who stared back without flinching.

"She never told me what she wanted to show me. I didn't kill her. I was…"

Barry placed a hand on Will's arm, and he shut his mouth.

"Your staff must like you very much because Wilma and Angi both said Janelle had come to the office screaming, making accusations, and you were calm and diffused the situation. They claimed. But I could see how that would make you angry. Want to hurt her before she could hurt your new girlfriend," Detective Clyde said.

Will's muscles tightened. "I didn't kill her."

"Tell me what you saw when you arrived at her house that morning."

"The front door was opened when I got there. I called out to her. There was no answer. I finally found her in her home office." He swallowed hard. "I…she was on the floor with a bullet to the chest. It was clean, one shot. I checked to see if she was alive and called the police immediately."

"Besides you, do you know who might want her dead?"

Will shook his head. "I haven't seen Janelle in four months. She started calling out of the blue, begging to talk, to get back together, threatening Nikki. I don't know what's been going on in her life. I don't know who she hung out with or what she did in her spare time. She divorced me. I was mad, sad, and relieved. I moved on."

Will whispered to Barry.

Barry nodded.

"What other evidence do you have that you think points to my client?" Barry asked.

Detective Clyde cleared his throat. "Janelle didn't keep much in her house. Just those letters."

"Very well. You've been interrogating my client for over an hour. On top of the three from a week ago. He has an alibi; there's no evidence he pulled the trigger. He has cooperated fully. We're done. Either throw him in jail and let me post bail or let him go."

Even though Will had been arrested, Detective Clyde didn't seem to get what he wanted from Will.

"You can leave the station, but do not leave the state," Detective Clyde ordered.

The detective left the room and Barry and Will followed. My stomach clinched fiercely, and I could barely breathe as I waited my turn.

What felt like hours as I waited and sweated in the nearly empty viewing room with two metal chairs and nothing else, made me even more anxious. When the door opened, I jumped in my seat. It was Barry.

"Will's waiting in the lobby. Let's get this over with."

He offered me a hand and led me next door.

It wasn't much better than the last room. Four chairs sat around a metal table. Not much else. I sat beside Barry. "This doesn't make sense," I whispered.

"No, it doesn't."

We both looked up as Benson Clyde walked in. He glanced at me, up and down stopping on my face. His gaze met mine.

He tossed the folder on the table and took a seat directly across from me. While I was still shaking, I sucked in some air and leaned forward, keeping my eyes on him. I wasn't going to let him get to me. I wasn't going to let him walk down the wrong investigative path. It wouldn't end well.

"Thank you for coming in, Mrs. Page. I need to know where you were the morning Janelle died, between seven and eight in the morning?" He proceeded to take out the crime scene photos and laid them across the table.

"I was at home getting ready for work and then at work by eight."

"Do you have someone who can confirm that?"

"That can be confirmed by Riley Houseman. She's the admin at the law firm I work for."

I watched him jot down notes in his small notebook.

When he finished, he glanced at me. "When was the last time you saw Janelle?"

"About two days before she died."

He waited for me to finish, but I had answered his question. He'd have to work harder for this one if he wanted more.

"Where was this?"

I thought back to that moment when she sneered at me while standing on my front porch. "She came to my house."

"Did you invite her there?"

"No." I touched my shaking leg to stop myself from moving.

Why was I so nervous?

"Why did she come over?"

I shrugged. "It's hearsay, and I can't give you a guess." I wasn't feeling cheeky, but Detective Clyde grimaced.

"Mrs. Page, what did she say to you?"

My heart pounded, and I couldn't stop trembling. I lay my hands in my lap. "She came over to tell me she was going to get Will back; he was her husband. She told me she didn't believe Will and I never had sex in all the years we were friends."

When he finished taking notes, he looked back at me. "Was this the first time she had come to your home?"

"Please be more specific," I said.

He cleared his throat and glared at me. "Mrs. Page, please answer my question."

"I've been friends with Will for over thirty years. We socialized as couples, multiple times during our marriages. She's been to my house before," I said emotionless. It was a poorly worded question which he now realized why.

"Since Janelle changed, was this the first time she was at your home?"

"Yes."

"You knew she had been calling Will and coming to his office?"

"Yes."

"How did that make you feel?"

Detective Clyde held his pen against his notepad, waiting expectantly for me to add what he thought would be the smoking gun, I'm sure. I wish I could have given it to him.

"I was concerned. She had been acting odd, and I have kids. That's why Will filed the restraining order."

"Was this behavior typical of Janelle?"

I rubbed my sweaty hands against my pant leg. "I haven't seen her in years. I don't know if this was typical of her recently."

Clyde shuffled through his notes, finding what he was looking for. "Will stated that Janelle began to act weird about three years ago. Asked for the divorce and then regretted it. And her behavior got worse. Is that your impression too?"

"Like I said, I haven't seen her in over three years. I hadn't seen Will in a few years either, for that matter. I was surprised by their divorce. But from what I knew about Janelle prior to all of this, I think something was going on in her life, and she might have been crying out for help."

He looked at me as if I said that thing he was after.

"What might have been going on in her life?"

"Ask Will, he'd know more about that than me. She wasn't acting typical. At least what I knew of her. Something was off, and you're looking at the wrong person."

"Did you know that Will spoke with Janelle's parents?"

I nodded. "I knew. He was worried about her. I was worried about her. Something was wrong."

"Why was he going there to see her?"

He was circling. I thought he was trying to get a rise out of me. I sighed. "Janelle begged him to come over. Wanted to discuss their relationship and getting back together. She asked for the divorce, and it wasn't an easy split, but Will moved on. He wanted to discuss it with her in person to get her to understand. Her parents called Will for help, he obliged because he still cared. The door was open when he got there. He found her dead. Will didn't do this. Look at someone else."

"Were you angry she was trying to take your fiancé?" Detective Clyde asked.

I bit my cheek to keep from laughing. The questions were ridiculous, designed to get a rise out of me. "I was not angry. I was worried and frustrated that she was doing this. But no, I wasn't angry she was trying to get Will back."

"You said you were at work when Janelle was killed. Did you want her dead?"

I opened my mouth but closed it when Barry placed his hand on mine.

"No, I didn't."

"You both claim she was acting odd. And yet you hadn't seen her in years. Maybe you and Will are telling me this to give the impression you cared. Did you come up with this scheme so you could off his ex-wife?"

Barry stood up so fast, I jumped. "Detective. Do your job, verify my client's alibi. Both of them have one. Unless you have evidence to the contrary, stop harassing my clients." Barry motioned me to follow him.

I walked ahead of him, my speed picking up when I exited the interrogation room. I was running when I reached the lobby.

Will stood when he saw me and came to me. I wrapped my arms around him.

"Are you okay?" Will whispered.

"That was…"

Barry held his hand up, and I quieted.

"I'm so sorry," he whispered.

"They're not holding you. You're free to go," Barry said.

"Are you ready to leave?" I asked.

He glanced around the lobby, nodding to his lawyer. "You have no idea."

CHAPTER 2

The silence in the car was deafening. Even if I knew what to say to Will, I wouldn't have said anything because there was nothing that would make this go away.

We both had to grieve Janelle's death, let the shock of her murder sink in, and find a way to muddle through what had happened to her. Understanding might make it easier.

I was lost in that thought when I pulled into the garage and turned off the car. Will made no attempt to exit. His gaze was empty, his jaw tight.

"Do they know?" Will couldn't look at me. I reached for his hand and he pulled it away.

"No. I ran from the house so fast when Barry called. I managed to text them that I didn't know when we'd be home."

I faced him. He had been crying and wiped his cheeks.

"This is nuts," he said. "I can't hide from them. Or this."

"Will, you have every right to be upset. Furious even. This has been far from rational."

"The letterhead doesn't prove anything. I have an alibi," he said angrily.

I leaned back in the driver's seat. "The letterhead goes to motive. Wildly grasping at a motive, but it fits whatever scenario they're trying to create. They let you go without bail because they know it's not enough. They know your alibi is solid."

His gaze turned toward the door to the laundry room. I sensed his apprehension in facing the kids. "What will you tell them?"

"They're old enough for the truth."

"I'm sorry." He hung his head while clutching the handle of his briefcase. One more swipe of tears from his cheek, and he opened the door.

"You've already apologized. You have nothing to be sorry for." I held his clammy hand. He was an emotional wreck, and I was unable to find the words to reassure him.

"She begged me to come over. I thought if I could talk to her in person, find out what's been going on…"

"Don't beat yourself up about this."

"I can't get past the guilt. If I knew something was wrong, I could've helped." He leaned back against the headrest. I lay my hand on his shoulder and kissed his cheek.

I wiped the tears from his cheeks. "Why don't you go upstairs, take a shower, climb into bed. I'll bring dinner up. It's been a long day."

He kissed me. It felt needy, like he was clinging to a lifeline. I knew he wouldn't get over this with kind words.

"Are you ready to go in?"

Will was more than rumpled, exhausted.

"Yeah. I'm ready to be home."

***

The house smelled delicious. Noodles cooked in the largest pot, while meatballs simmered in sauce.

Jacob placed the plates on the island, while Emily took out garlic bread from the oven. Julia stirred the sauce that almost boiled over.

"Mom, Will…" Emily began happily and stopped at our overall expressions. "What happened?"

Jacob and Julia stopped what they were doing and glanced at us. I nodded to Will who grimaced as he walked through kitchen on his way upstairs without saying a word.

"Mom. What happened?" Jacob asked.

I held up my hand to ask them to wait as I listened for his footsteps to reach the top of the stairs. When the door closed, I met Jacob's gaze. "He was arrested today."

"What?" Julia screeched.

I held up my hands. "They let him go without bail. The evidence they found wasn't enough to hold him."

"What happened? How did this happen?" Emily asked.

"They're investigating. They found what they thought was motive. They arrested him but there's nothing to hold him. The alibi is solid. Whoever murdered Janelle had time to take the weapon with them. If it was Will, he wouldn't have had enough time. They're ignoring the evidence."

I glanced at the ceiling, below my bedroom, and heard the spaghetti sauce boiling over.

"Shit," I said as I turned off the flame and stirred the sauce. I noticed the meatballs and realized how hungry I was.

"Is he gonna be, okay?" Julia asked.

"Give him time. He was at the police station for a few hours today, not to mention the three hours a few days ago. And he's still mourning Janelle. It's a lot."

I returned to the food, tested a piece of spaghetti and pulled the strainer from the water straining the noodles. "Looks like dinner's ready."

The kids grabbed their plates and waited patiently for space to plate their food.

"Is Will coming down?" Jacob asked.

I held the empty plate. "He needs to process everything. I'll get him dinner and leave him be." I plated his dinner. "I'll be down in a bit."

"I know this is a lot, but we're family. He doesn't have to hide," Jacob said.

"He knows. It's been a long day. Give him time."

***

I placed his dinner on the bedside table while Will was in the walk-in closet changing. He came out in a t-shirt and shorts, and he still looked rumpled.

"Thanks. I'm starving."

He sat on the bed, took the plate in his lap, but didn't dig in. "Are the kids okay?" he asked.

"They're concerned. Jacob wanted me to let you know it's okay. You can come down. We're family."

It was the first smile of the afternoon. "For tonight, I'd like to stay up here."

There had been something nagging at me since I saw those letters at the police station. I couldn't let go of the question that needed asking. "I don't want to harp on this, but I'm curious about something."

He looked up. "Ask."

"If Janelle asked you to write those letters, would you have?"

He rubbed his hands across his chin as if he had to think of the answer. I figured he knew why I was asking. He had written a letter for me when I asked.

"I'm sorry, I had to ask."

Will put the plate on the table and stood. He was restless and began pacing the short width of the room. "There's a difference between a simple request asking a photographer for a model release and asking an insurance company to circumvent the law."

His voice dripped with anger, and I was surprised by the nature of the letters. No wonder the police asked him to come back in, even though the letters went to motive.

He didn't stop pacing, rather he began walking the length of the room, his arms waving around himself as he spoke. "Yes, I could research it, I could have written the letters for Janelle, but what she was asking of the insurance companies was more complex and required knowledge of insurance law. From what I could see in those letters, there were complicated legal requirements that she was asking the company to waive."

While my bedroom wasn't small, it wasn't so large. Will's pacing became faster, angrier. I wondered if the kids could hear the stomping and what they were thinking.

"What the hell was she thinking?" he said angrily.

He stopped at the window and looked outside to the empty street. His breathing was raspy and rough. His fingers tapped on the window sill nervously.

"Wouldn't the center have a legal team to handle difficult patient issues?"

He looked at me. "Yes. If not inhouse, they'd have a law firm or a few they regularly worked with." He left the spot by the window, and walked past me and re-entered the closet, coming back out with a hoodie on. "If she needed help with a patient, I could have recommended someone with insurance knowledge. But whatever firm the center had could have handled it."

"She was hiding what she was doing from the center's legal firm," I reminded him.

"That's exactly what she did and used my good name in her scheme," he said bitterly.

"The only reason to go behind someone's back is because she knew what she was doing was illegal," I said.

He had entered the bathroom and splashed water on his face. He turned, dripping water from his hands and face. "What did she get herself into?"

I grabbed a towel and dried his face. "When did her uncharacteristic behavior start?"

He leaned against the sink. "Everything changed about three years ago."

"You told the police that."

He nodded. "I did."

"So, rationally, the police will look at the timeline and try to figure out what happened three years ago that changed Janelle. Was it the fertility treatments that led to the affair, that led to whatever she got herself into?"

He shrugged. "I don't know."

"The police will find out. That's their job."

"She forged letters to insurance companies. It reeks of insurance fraud. I can't figure how infertility led to that," he said.

I put my arms around his neck. "How about this? I can do a little digging. If I find something, I find something. Maybe help the police." I touched his cheek, stood on tippy toes and kissed him.

"Thank you," he said when he pulled away.

He ran his fingers through his short hair. "Barry's going to hire a forensics computer specialist to prove the letters weren't written or printed from any of my computers. In case the police decide to revisit that."

I nodded. "They have a theory, and it's a sound theory. Wrong but sound. They think she got you into something illegal and you killed her because of it. Anything to help prove the police theory is wrong can't hurt."

It was the second smile this afternoon. He wrapped me in his arms.

"Thank you. I couldn't do this without you."

I squeezed my arms around him. "By the way, they never found the gun, did they?"

Will shook his head. "No. They did ask me during the first interrogation where I hid it. I told them I didn't shoot the gun, and I have no idea where the murder weapon is."

Will glanced at his phone. "I have work I need to do since I was out most of the day. Wilma sent me several emails about issues and rescheduled client appointments. Tell the kids thanks for dinner, and I appreciate their support, but I'm gonna stay up here for the night."

"You take care of what you need to. I'll deal with the kids."

I kissed his cheek and let him be.

As I walked down the stairs, there was something I haven't heard in a while from my kids. They were discussing something in harsh tones.

"Stay out of it," Emily growled as I entered the kitchen.

"He's an ass. Be thankful he broke up with you," Jacob said.

"Excuse me. I could hear the two of you bickering from upstairs. What's up?"

"Marshall broke up with Emily, and Jacob's happy about it. Emily's pissed," Julia said as she took a bite of a meatball.

"Oh. I'm sorry he broke up with you," I said to Emily. She wiped tears from her cheek.

I touched her shoulder.

"He was a jerk. She's lucky he's gone," Jacob said.

I turned toward my son and glared at him. "Leave her alone. A break up is still hard."

I plated my own food and sat with the kids. "Will thanks you for dinner. He needs some time to catch up on some things." I took a bite of the meatball. It was either very good or I was very hungry.

The kids on the other hand were playing with the food on their plates. "Everything else okay today?" I asked. There was more to their disagreement than they were letting on.

"Everything is fine," Emily snapped. She wrapped the spaghetti around her fork and nibbled on the pasta.

Jacob scooped up the meatball and took it in one bite.

Julia slurped spaghetti through her teeth.

Some things never changed.

"I feel like you're not telling me everything about what's going on with you two. I'm not gonna press, but if you want to talk, I'll be here."

Neither said anything or looked at each other, their anger was still front and center, I'd let them come to me if they felt like it, hoping they would.

It was an awkward silence as we ate.

I looked up when I heard my name. "Mom?" Emily had a serious expression on her face.

"What's up?" I asked hopefully.

"You're gonna investigate Janelle's murder, right?" Emily asked.

She turned toward the hallway. Will was standing there.

"Your mom's busy. She'll look into what she can," Will said.

He was right. There was so much going on, and yet, I couldn't drop it. I knew I'd be looking into Janelle's murder and find the spaces she tried too hard to hide.

"I'll dig a little but it feels intrusive to dig into Janelle's life."

"You helped Penelope," Emily said.

"I did. But I wasn't friends with Penelope, and I'm engaged to Janelle's ex-husband. It's a little different."

"But, Mom. You're really good at it. You solved cold cases. You should do this," Emily said.

Flattery. Why?

"Hmmm. Keep me busy so I don't have to worry about the two of you?"

"Well, if I wanted that, I'd use a different approach. I think you should investigate, though," Emily began. She pushed something at me.

It was a pile of bridal magazines.

"I'm not sure if now's the right time," I said.

Will shrugged. "Maybe we should pick a date at least."

"Winter break?" I asked.

"I was thinking August. Before school," Will said.

I shook my head. "Don't you think it's too soon. You're ex-wife…"

He held up his hand. "It might be. But I want something to look forward to. Think about it. Otherwise, December works."

"If you investigate Janelle's death and get her justice, you can move forward," Emily said.

I picked up the first magazine. Emily had noted several pages with sticky notes. I perused the pages, glanced at tablescapes, chairs, flowers, the dresses. It would be so nice to plan and prepare for something happy. We had spent so many months entrenched in cases, searching for people, and helping others at their most vulnerable. It was time for us to take center stage.

But Janelle's murder…

"I want to pick a date. But with Janelle's murder…"

"If you're really concerned about that now, let's do December. Go on a family honeymoon and then you and I can go away a few months later," Will said.

"Let's do that! Can we go to Disney?" Julia asked.

I was surprised when Julia ran to Will and hugged him. Emily and Jacob followed. I knew my kids liked him quite a bit, but this was overwhelming. I could tell it was for Will as well, when tears welled in his eyes.

"I guess they like that plan," I said.

"I appreciate the support from you all. I promise, I didn't kill my ex-wife. We'll get through this."

Will looked at me when he said that. I nodded.

"Great." Emily took out another magazine. "Now that we're all happy, I had some ideas." She pulled out another magazine. "I thought Jules and I could wear these." She handed me the picture of two young women wearing light blue, full length dresses.

"Uh uh. No way," Julia said and rolled her eyes.

"Come on, Jules. They're pretty," Emily argued.

"I appreciate you looking into this honey, but dresses need to be ordered almost a year in advance. Let's go shopping in a few weeks, and you can pull something off the racks appropriate for the wedding. Think small and intimate," I said.

"Okay. I can work with that. Jules and I can go. We'll find something."

"Why can't I wear jeans? It's not fancy." Julia asked.

"Can we compromise? We'll go shopping in two weeks. And we'll find something all of us will be happy with. Okay?" I glanced at both of them with my most serious mom face. Neither of my daughters were intimidated by it.

"Sure mom. Two weeks," Emily said.

Again, Julia rolled her eyes, and for a moment, things felt normal.

***

Will, with his computer in his lap, caught up on hundreds of emails he missed over the three hours he sat at the police station. He read, took notes, and looked things up. I didn't figure he'd finish until morning.

Leaving him to his work, I turned to my computer and pulled up my favorite databases. But my fingers hovered above the keyboard.

Did I really want to insert myself into Janelle's murder investigation? Even though my kids believed in my abilities to investigate, I still hesitated. Without contacts in the police department, I knew I'd be up against a concrete wall. But most importantly, I had known Janelle for years. I felt too close to the victim and her ex-husband. I glanced at Will, entrenched in a new email, his mouth twitching as he read his screen.

I typed Janelle Dixon Mann in the search box. Let the first query run. In the meantime, I picked up my purse and cleaned it out, first tossing the visitor's pass from the police department and then finding the hand addressed letter I found in the mail pile today.

"Lose something?" Will asked as he stared in my direction.

"No. I found this letter for me in the mail pile."

I ripped it open and pulled out the scrap of a note inside. "Oh," I said as I read.

Nikki,

I can't apologize enough for what I've put you and Will through over the last several months. It wasn't my intention to cause further pain. But I find myself in a very bad situation.

I made some bad choices, and now I'm in serious trouble. I need your help, Nikki. I don't know how else to get out of this situation.

If you could find forgiveness, I'd really like to meet with you. I need you to look at something. It's important.

Janelle

"What's the matter?" Will asked.

I handed Will the note.

He read it and possibly re-read it. His jaw clenched and released several times before handing the letter back to me. "When did this come?"

I shrugged. "It's dated a few days before she died. I'm not sure when it came though. I found it in the mail pile this afternoon."

"She knew she was in trouble but thought she had time."

I sat beside him. "I think she hired me."

He chuckled. "Do you have enough time for a big investigation?"

"I'll start with the basic queries and see where it takes me. I feel like I'm too close to the situation, but I'm almost done with Samuel Ross, and I do need investigative hours for the PI license, and I have no job in two weeks."

"Thank you. From me and from Janelle."

I touched his arm. He gave me one last look, sighed and returned to his work.

The search queries I ran were basic to give myself an idea of her professional life online, or even her personal life that she herself put out there. I wasn't expecting anything as I read through the results.

I felt Will's gaze on me, and I reviewed the basic results. Her job, address, social media notifications, and then…

"Well, hell." I looked at Will.

"What?"

I turned the computer screen toward him. "I… I didn't know this? How did I not know she lost her license."

"A person loses a license if they maliciously act against the standard operating procedures that guide their field."

"I can't believe Janelle would act in an egregious manner," Will said.

I grabbed my computer and pulled up Murphy Speech Therapy Center where Janelle worked. "Okay. First thing, she's already been taken off of the work website." I switched websites and pulled up the American Speech-Language-

Hearing Association website but couldn't find any explanation as to why she lost her license. All I could find was that she lost her license and her name was moved to the do not hire list.

What would cause a person to lose a license? Insurance fraud was first and foremost on my mind so I searched for lawsuits. If it was that bad, someone would have been pissed. I hit pay dirt immediately.

"Okay. Here it is." I clicked on the link to the lawsuit. "Janelle, another person named George Egan, and the Murphy Speech Therapy clinic were sued," I turned the computer to Will.

He perused the document and pulled up several of the attached exhibits.

"According to this, the parents of a three-year-old patient claim she gave the wrong diagnosis for their kid. They claim it caused a permanent delay for their son. Which might not be true." He followed the link trail through the documents. "I'm not a doctor or speech therapist but the supporting evidence seems to prove their claims."

I went back to the query results and started pulling up various data. "Okay. The lawsuit was filed ten months ago. According to the evidence, she was fired four months ago and three months ago, she lost her license."

Will leaned against the headboard. "From a lawyer's perspective, I interpret that as the lawsuit was filed and in the course of discovery and depositions, a critical piece of information was discovered. It was probably bad enough to fire her, and bad enough that the Murphy's clinic felt it needed to have her license revoked. Do we know if George Egan lost his job too?"

I went back to the clinic's website. George Egan wasn't on the site either.

I returned to the American Speech-Language-Hearing Association and found George had lost his license too. "Neither are working at the clinic, and they both lost their license."

"The family was already suing her, so I suspect they didn't kill her. They'd rather have justice in the form of monetary compensation. I did see they were asking for $500,000 claiming their son would need extra care," Will said. He closed his eyes and rubbed his temples.

"What if Janelle got George fired because of what she did, and he killed her as retribution?" I suggested.

"I spent time with him at business functions. He was a mousy man. A little uptight. He doesn't exactly fit the murderer type," Will said.

"And there's a murderer type?"

Will glanced at me and grimaced. "No. I suppose not. But knowing all of that, it explains her behavior. Coming at me. She must have been desperate."

"What would you have done if she wasn't killed? If she told you what happened?"

"I would have tried to help her. Legal help, found her a lawyer, helped with money. But I wouldn't have gotten back together with her, if that's what you're worried about."

I shook my head. I really wasn't worried about that. "No. That wasn't a question. I was more curious than anything."

Will pulled his notebooks together and put them in his briefcase. "I'm done for the night. I'll get back to it in the morning." He shut down his computer and slid it in his bag. "I appreciate you finding out what you have. And I'd like you to keep digging, but not at the expense of your PI license."

I looked at him confused. "Are you sure? I still have questions. Did this scheme or whatever it was, start three years ago? How many other insurance issues did she have? Those forged letters are still a problem for me."

Will took my hands. "After the last case. After almost losing you to Ethan, I'm worried. This is huge. A huge scheme or plan. But it can't be good and the more I think about it, the more I worry about you. This gives me an idea, but I'm afraid of what else is out there to learn. And I need to fully mourn her and move on before we get married. I need some time before that happens."

"I'm good with that. I have a PI to get my apprentice hours. If I can, I'll use this as part of the training. I want to make sure the right person is put away. I have time. And I'll be careful."

Will sighed. "I would have helped her if she told me."

I shut down my computer, placed it on the chair. "I know. Maybe even saved her."

We readied for bed in silence, and I turned off the lights, climbed into bed. Will wrapped me in his arms. "I love you. I love our life. I'm sorry this is happening."

I turned toward him. He kissed me, and in the darkness, where our fears and anxieties were hidden, he and I made love. It felt as though he was trying too hard to move on. I thought it might be fear. Fear of the truth, of what we would find if I kept digging. In a way, I didn't think Will wanted to know what Janelle had gotten herself into. But I couldn't let it rest.

And for me, the lovemaking was my attempt to shield him, if just for a moment, from any additional pain.

CHAPTER 3

The kitchen island was covered in work, mine and Will's nearly intermingling. I was organizing the pages I had printed the previous evening, sorting them into different folders. Will had been stuffing his documents into his work bag and stopped when he saw the lawsuit against Janelle and the speech therapy center.

He picked it up and perused it again, shuffling through the pages, stopping on the evidence, and moving on again, periodically clearing his throat or letting a quiet moan out as he realized the extent of what Janelle had done.

We knew more today than we did yesterday. She was committing insurance fraud, and we had only touched the tip of the iceberg. And as a result of a misdiagnosis, Janelle was sued alongside her boss George Egan and both of the former speech therapists had lost their licenses as a result.

From what Will had said, Janelle's demeanor changed about three years ago. If I were to look into this case, I needed to find out what happened during that time period. Either what happened led her to the insurance fraud, or the insurance fraud led her to the personality changes. I couldn't imagine what it would take for me to enter into illegal activities.

Will clenched his jaw as he re-read the lawsuit. He made notes in the margins. When he had enough, he slid the document to me.

"What's the plan for today?" Will asked. The monotone cadence to his voice was off putting and so unlike him. Yesterday had worn him down.

"Work this morning. I have a few boxes to send out."

I took the lawsuit and placed it in a folder in my work bag.

"How's your day shaping up?" I asked him. With the shadow of the arrest, the presumption of guilt hanging over him, I wondered how that would affect his relationship with his staff and if it would affect how his clients saw him. Today wouldn't be a good day.

He took a sip of his coffee. "Catching up from yesterday." There was just enough anger in his voice. He tried hard to mask it.

"Wilma and Angi will help you through it," I said as I closed the zipper on my bag.

"It shouldn't have happened. They shouldn't have arrested me." The bitterness dripped in his words. What had happened could have affected his job and relationship with his clients or the courts. It still might.

"It kept me up last night."

I touched his cheek. His flesh was warm. "I'm sorry."

Will held my hand, kissed my palm. "You shouldn't be sorry. This isn't your fault. It's mine. I should have asked more questions. Figured out what was happening to her. I could have handled the situation better."

I hugged him. He felt tight against me as his whole body was taut with stress.

"They won't completely rule me out," he said.

"You didn't do this. Someone else did. You're mourning and caught in the middle because it often is the spouse or ex-spouse."

"What will I lose in all of this? My clients? I already lost Janelle. I can't lose you. Or the kids."

"We're not going anywhere. You didn't kill her, and the police know it. They let you go because they don't have any evidence. They'll drop the charges. We will get through this."

He sunk his chin against my shoulder. "Thank you." He pulled away and swung his work bag over his shoulder. "If the day isn't horrendous like I fear it will be, maybe dinner out tonight?"

"That's a good idea. Let's see how your day goes."

I could see the sleepless night in his eyes. When he smiled, his eyes were empty.

"I love you," he said.

"I love you," I responded.

He walked away, dejected, hurting and helpless. It strengthened my resolve as I looked at the piles I had accumulated regarding Janelle's life before her death. The things we didn't know, the secrets she successfully hid.

While it felt so much like voyeurism because she had once been a friend, I knew I needed to start where it all began for her. That three-year period of time. Knowing where it was heading, I left for work.

My morning passed quickly.

From the minute I arrived, I spent the time with Riley, coordinating several different boxes of files for four different law firms. At lunch, Riley told me she found another job. While that might leave me alone to finish, I was happy she found something else. I hoped I'd be so lucky.

I was looking forward to the quiet of home when I left the office four hours later. I had studying to do, and investigating Janelle's murder, and I assumed the kids were off and running as usual.

Unfortunately, quiet and solitude was not what I found.

I heard the yelling as soon as I pulled into the garage and that was through the closed house door. I opened it, the screeching was so unlike my children. I assumed it was part of their overall discourse I had heard the other night.

"But that's not fair!" Emily yelled.

"He's an idiot, can't you see it?" Jacob shouted back.

"He's not an idiot. He screwed up," Emily argued.

"Stop it!" Julia's shrieking voice shut them all up. She was crying.

"What the hell is going on?" I asked.

Emily had been crying, Jacob was red in the face, Julia came to me and buried her head in my chest. "What is going on?" I demanded.

"It's…" Emily looked at Jacob and lowered her gaze, embarrassed maybe.

"Marshall's still hanging around and stringing her along. We're having friends over tonight, and I told her she can't invite him. He's mean and teased Jules so bad she was crying. I can't stand the guy."

I had only met Marshall a few times and had no real opinion of him. I felt a little out of the picture and that bothered me. Also, this new information angered me.

"Why didn't you tell me you were having issues with him?" I asked.

“I didn’t tell you because of all the shit you’ve gone through lately. I’m not getting back together with him, and he’s not stringing me along. We do have fun together. I didn’t think it was fair that I couldn’t invite him,” Emily said quietly.

I looked at my kids. “What the hell is the matter with you? You don’t fight, not like this. I could hear you when I shut off my car. What’s really going on?”

“Marshall cheated on her. She forgave him. They’re both idiots,” Jacob said.

I looked from Jacob to Emily and planted my feet to support myself rather than lean on Julia. “Okay. Listen. Jacob, it’s Emily’s life. Support her. If you disagree, tell her and move on. But don’t call her an idiot. And I’m sure this feels close to home because of Dad and me. Meaning you need to understand forgiveness.”

“Why should she forgive him?”

“First of all, it’s Emily’s thing, not yours. Secondly, forgiveness doesn’t mean you absolve the person who wronged you. You forgive them in order to release the anger you carry around regarding that thing they’ve done to hurt you.”

“So, you forgive for you, not them,” Julia said.

“Yes.”

“Have you forgiven Dad?” Emily asked.

“I have.” All three of the kids seemed shocked by that. “I forgave your dad so I could let go of the anger I’ve held on to.

I no longer hate him; I no longer hate Amber. Yes, he hurt us, and she was complicit in that. But living with that anger was harmful to me and to you. I held onto it for three years, and I won't hang on to it anymore. And you Emily, you're young. If he cheated now, he'll do it again. Forgive him, release the anger and don't see him again."

I turned to Jacob. "And you. While I appreciate your attempt to protect your sister, leave her alone. She'll figure out what she needs to figure out on her own."

They stood there stunned by my diatribe, though it wasn't a surprise revelation. At least, I didn't think it was.

I kissed Julia on the forehead and turned my attention to the pantry and pulled out cans of tuna for sandwiches.

"You really forgave Dad?"

"Yeah. I did. I also said fuck it. And because of that, I finally moved on. I can't tell you how to mourn the loss of your relationship with your father, or how to deal with Amber and Brayden, but he wants to work on it. Forgive him, dump the anger and move on. And try to support each other."

"You're an ass," Emily said to Jacob. "I'm not getting back together with him. He's an ass." She smiled and wiped her eyes.

"Just don't be a dummy where Mr. Dumbass is concerned. Everyone saw him for what he was."

He tried to smile but crinkled his eyebrows in thought.

I mixed tuna with mayo as they talked. I wondered if my outside activities brought on more stress into the house.

"Are you okay otherwise?" I asked as I licked my fork. I was starving.

"Yeah, why?" Jacob asked.

"With Will and all the other things lately. It's a lot. I know it is."

"Janelle coming here and Will being arrested scared us. Maybe more than we thought," Emily admitted. "You think that's why we're fighting?"

"I don't know. It's the screaming, and Jules's reaction. You guys don't fight like that. It's like all of the outside stress is causing stress inside. Let me protect you from that so you can just be yourselves. Please."

"I guess it has been a lot," Emily said.

I nodded. "Let's eat lunch, and you two try to resolve your issues with a little less shouting, please?"

They both nodded.

"As long as we shout softly, you'll be okay," Jacob joked.

"Yes, funny man. As long as you argue in harsh whispers, I'll be fine."

The kids smiled, and we ate lunch rather quietly, each thinking our own thoughts.

CHAPTER 4

At the beginning of summer, I watched the kids spend time together, usually running off in one direction. It was disconcerting as they headed out in three different directions. Probably fairly normal and understandable, but their wall of protection seemed to be cracking.

At their ages, there was nothing I could do except remind them to be kind and try to find a solution. It wasn't as simple as that.

I left the house, my intention to learn what happened to Janelle and George Egan at the speech therapy center. I wanted to know why Janelle was fired, what was George Egan's involvement, who else knew what was going on, what did they know, and what did they do?

My thoughts swirled as I entered the full parking lot for the medical building that housed the Murphy Speech Therapy Center and several other doctor's offices. I found the last open spot at the far end of the lot. I pulled in, turned off the car and grabbed my bag. I crossed the lot and headed to the one story, office building that from the board in the foyer, housed six different doctor's offices. I found Murphy's on the information board and walked down the hallway toward the office. The speech therapy clinic was behind double glass doors that led into a light and airy reception area.

The receptionist named Teddi Hanson looked up when I entered.

"Hi. I'm Nikki Page. I'm a private investigator, investigating the murder of Janelle Mann. Can you answer a few questions for me?"

Teddi's dark brown eyes widened; her face blanched. The stark contrast between the dark eyes and pale skin gave her a sick pallor. My heart sped up because something in that question and more importantly, the answers I sought, made her anxious.

"I don't think I can answer any questions. Excuse me. I'll find someone who can."

She raced into the nearest office and closed the door behind her. A family walked in, sat in the waiting area. I smiled as I tapped my fingers against the reception desk. Minutes ticked away, and I tried a new position while standing. Finally, Teddi returned to her post.

"Mrs. Page, follow me."

I was escorted to the manager's office. From what Will told me, that should have been George Egan, but he had been fired after Janelle.

The woman behind the desk was named Debra Lerner, and she smiled when I entered. She folded her hands on the table top and I took her in. The coiffed hair, not a strand out of place, her off white suit impeccably pressed and clean.

"Mrs. Page. You're here about Janelle?"

I nodded. "Yes. I'm investigating her murder. I was hoping you could explain why she was fired and was it related to the lawsuit against Murphy Speech Therapy Center? Also, who was responsible for having her license revoked?"

Her eye twitched, and her smile waned. "I see you did your research."

"It's my job." She hadn't offered, but I sat across from her. I took out my notebook and pen and waited for Debra to answer.

She fumbled with the pile of folders on her desk as she straightened them. "Yes. Well, Janelle was fired because she was coming to work late, bringing her personal problems to work. She was misdiagnosing patients, so much so that one patient case led to the lawsuit as you've seen."

I waited for Debra to look me in the eyes. Her gaze remained on her pile of documents. I knew she was either lying or holding something back.

After writing my few notes I believed were pure bullshit, I looked back at Debra, still fiddling with something on her desk. This time, a pen.

"Was that enough to warrant termination?" I asked. Employees sometimes had personal issues but weren't fired for their troubles. And even with the lawsuit, their legal team could have worked through it and retained Janelle.

Debra's hand trembled. She noticed my gaze and placed them in her lap. "It was worth termination. The lawsuit wasn't the only misdiagnosis. Yes, she had problems, could have asked for help, but she didn't. She missed work, cancelled on patients. We had no choice but to let her go."

I made another note. "Was the lawsuit the reason she lost her license?"

Debra grimaced. "Well, yes. At least in part. She had an obligation to the patients and to this office. She was not honoring that obligation or following any professional code of ethics."

"An ethics violation is a heavy accusation. Can you give me some examples?"

She shook her head. "I can't," she said. "I'm not at liberty to discuss that with anyone."

"I understand," I said. I really did. There might have been a gag order placed on this case due to the lawsuit. I wasn't going to fight that.

"About the license termination. Was it someone here at the office who requested it?"

Debra shook quickly. "I wasn't in this position when Janelle was fired and her license suspended. I'm assuming it was someone in the office as it should have been."

"You replaced George Egan, correct?"

Debra nodded. "I think I've answered enough."

"I think the police are going to be a lot harder on you when they come here asking questions."

She looked at me.

"Why was George let go? He lost his license as well."

Debra pulled out a folder, opened it and closed it again. I watched as she stood, walked to the office window and kept her gaze outside.

"George and Janelle had many questionable claims. I haven't seen them, this is hearsay, I suppose," Debra explained. She remained by the window; her eyes trained on something outside.

"When were the claims discovered?"

"During discovery and the depositions for the lawsuit. It all came out. I don't think they would have been fired for the lawsuit, but the claims."

"Janelle filed the claims. What was George's role in this?"

"He approved them. He should have seen what she was doing. He was either stupid or in on whatever she was doing."

This time, Debra turned, her arms crossed against her chest.

"How long was this going on? These questionable claims?"

"I don't know for sure. Somewhere around two or two and a half years. It had been going on for a while. No one knew."

My thought was, for this lawsuit, the plaintiff's lawyer most likely only requested Janelle's claims, since the lawsuit was against Janelle and George, but it was also the therapy center.

"Did the plaintiff's team look at claims from other therapists?"

Debra looked anywhere but at me. "I don't know what they looked at."

If they had looked at claims filed by other therapists, my guess was, the plaintiffs would have evidence against the other therapists at the center. I couldn't believe Janelle was the only one who had a part in the claim's fraud case.

I glanced at my notes. "Do you have a billing department?"

"Of course, why?"

"Doesn't billing have to verify and code claims?"

"I suppose, yes."

"How many work in billing?"

"Just one. Martha Hartman. She didn't know. Her affidavit is part of the lawsuit," Debra said quickly.

After taking the last of my notes, I stood. "Thank you for your time." I wrote my name on a page of my notebook with my phone number and ripped it from the book. I handed it to Debra. "If you remember anything else, please let me know."

She stared at the handwritten contact information. "Are you sure you're a PI?"

"I'm a paralegal and I investigate cases for lawyers. I'll be taking my licensure test in two months. Sorry I wasn't honest. But I am investigating for the police."

Debra sat at the desk, pulled open the desk drawer and found a folder. She passed it to me. "If it makes a difference, Janelle was a good therapist, and I liked her a lot."

I opened the folder. It looked to be Janelle's Human Resources file.

"What happened to change everything?"

Debra shrugged. "Things changed. I don't know what happened that changed her. I know she was having trouble getting pregnant and trouble with Will at times. It wasn't just this year. It went farther back than that."

"Do you know when her troubles started?"

"Two or three years ago, I think. We don't know exactly when she started with the insurance fraud or if that's what started the problems, but we had several conversations with her over the last year or so warning her about the possibility she could lose her job if she didn't get it together."

"I know this is hard for everyone. Will and I have been shocked and upset," I said.

She looked at me, her eyebrows wide with surprise. "You know Janelle and Will?"

"I've known Will since college, and Janelle for about eighteen years."

"Isn't that a conflict of interest?"

I thought of that. It probably wasn't the most ethical, but I couldn't help thinking of Janelle's request to me. Maybe Debra was right and it was a conflict, but I didn't owe her the reason why I was doing this. "Janelle reached out to me before she died. And Will asked me to work with the police."

"How is he? I know she asked for the divorce, but he was so nice, so sweet. He must be devastated."

"He's understandably upset. He just wants to find peace for her. Anyway, I've taken up too much of your time. Thank you for the information."

I left her office. The receptionist saw me and turned toward her work, ignoring me. The waiting area was empty.

I let myself out and headed home. There was that two-to-three-year period when everything started. I had Will's remembrance but now I thought I needed to contact Janelle's friends to see what they knew.

I also knew I'd have to return to the speech therapy center because Debra wasn't telling me the whole truth.

***

Emily and Jacob's cars were gone, giving me a respite from their fight. I found Julia's note, telling me she was at the beach with Minnie.

All alone!

A little worn from my conversation with Debra, I made myself a tea and collected all my research for Janelle's murder.

Will had given me a list of Janelle's friends and their phone numbers. I glanced at my phone it was after five. Maybe someone would be willing to talk to me.

I started with Kristy McDonald, Janelle's self-proclaimed best friend, a woman I've met several times over the years. The first time I met her, she was Janelle's maid of honor, and I was just Will's friend from college. And because of that, there had always been a strain between us at barbecues, pot lucks and restaurant dinners over the years.

I wasn't sure how much she'd tell me, but I thought buttering her up might give her incentive.

"Hello…" she asked with confusion and sadness in her voice.

"Hi Kristy, this is Nikki Page. I'm friends with Will. We've met several times over the years."

"Um… yeah. I know you. This isn't a good time. Can we talk later?" she said tersely.

"Kristy, I know it's a hard time, but I'm investigating Janelle's murder, and I was hoping you had time to talk."

She snorted and laughed. "You? You're investigating Janelle's murder? I can save you the trouble. It's that fiancé of yours. Tossed her away and moved on really fast," she said.

I held my breath and counted to ten. "I'm very sorry for your loss. Janelle's death has been a shock for everyone. Including Will."

"Was it really a shock for you and Will?" she said angrily.

I wasn't exactly sure where her anger toward Will and I was coming from, unless Janelle had told her something.

"I'm sorry if these questions upset you, but Janelle was going through something. I want to make sure her killer is found."

"Right. You want to find out who killed Janelle so your fiancé will be cleared, and you can get married or whatever. You're tacky and disgusting."

I had expected her to hang up with all that anger dripping from her words, but I could hear her tapping something against a hard element.

"I'm not sure what you think you know, but Janelle was acting differently years before the divorce. Something was seriously wrong with her. Your anger towards me isn't going to help find her killer. You can either answer some questions or you can hang up. Either way, I'll find out who killed her because it wasn't Will, and it wasn't me. And while you're still on the phone, she cheated on him, and she asked for the divorce. Anything else is a lie."

I couldn't help defending him. I felt my heart speeding up, and it was hard to take a breath.

"Unbelievable," she muttered.

"What did Janelle tell you?" I finally asked when I could breathe without huffing and puffing in anger.

Kristy stopped tapping. "She… told me he cheated on her with you, actually."

I laughed. I couldn't help it. There might have been something between Will and I over the years. Feelings buried deep that were never acted on. It didn't matter now.

"No. That didn't happen," I said.

"You're a liar. I can't believe you and Will never…"

"I met my husband when I was twenty. I married him at twenty-four. And before that, Will and I never were together. Believe it or not. But either way, the truth was, Janelle cheated, and she changed. She asked for the divorce. It won't change what happened to her, but finding her killer will help her rest in peace."

"You're lying," she said quietly.

I was still surprised that she hadn't hung up yet.

"If you think about Janelle over the last three years, really think about what was going on with her, you'd see that what she told you was all a lie."

"Of course you'd say that. Janelle was struggling after the divorce, angry and bitter. She couldn't believe he did it… cheat on her like she had done…" her voice grew soft, like she remembered something.

"She had done?" I asked.

She didn't answer right away. She sighed deeply.

"What happened?" I asked.

"I… I don't know what to say. She told a different story. I can't believe she would have lied so badly. What did she get herself into?"

"I don't know. That's why I'm asking. Can you tell me what she had done?"

She was quiet for a moment and then said, "They had a magical life, but you're right, she did start acting differently. Scattered, angry, keeping secrets. She did tell me about a secret affair she had. I wasn't surprised. That was something Janelle would do, not Will."

"She cheated on him before this?"

"Not on Will. On a previous boyfriend. But we were in college and young and stupid. But I really thought she did this because Will had done something to her, and she was retaliating."

"Why would you think that? What did she say to you?" I had to speak slowly. I was getting tired of the accusations on behalf of Will.

"I shouldn't be talking to you. I feel like I'm betraying Janelle."

"Listen Kristy. You're not betraying Janelle by helping find her killer. If she did something, angered the wrong person, we need to know. The police will want to know."

"I'm… I'm just surprised you called me. I'm pissed at Janelle and Will for what happened. They were the couple I aspired to. And now he's moved on. And you're the one who's investigating. She had me convinced he was the bad guy. I just don't know what to do."

I wanted to face palm. "Kristy. If you know anything about Janelle's life, about what was going on, it can help. Either tell me or call the police and let them know what you know."

"I can't. I can't do this right now. It's too soon and you're with Will and it's so…"

The line went dead.

For now, I'd put this in the column that Kristy was upset about Janelle's death. Maybe I'd revisit this conversation or maybe I'd rethink my strategy. I put down my phone and lay against the sofa, closing my eyes. Kristy was angry, Janelle had lied to her. And now she's remembered something. For so long, everything had been so mixed up and yet no one knew something was seriously going on. Not until Janelle died. Maybe it's guilt.

Since I didn't get anything else from her, I moved on to the next friend on the list.

After contacting Sydney Rider, someone I had never met before, she agreed to meet, and I picked what became my favorite café in Lake Zurich in which to meet during an investigation.

The café was empty even though it was 5:45 in the evening. I found myself hungry and ordered a slice of pie and a tea as I waited for Sydney to arrive.

A woman my age entered the restaurant. She looked around, spotted me, and waved before coming over. She stopped at the table. "Nikki Page?"

I nodded and motioned for her to sit. "Thanks for agreeing to meet me."

"Anything to help find Janelle's killer. I never believed Will would have killed her. Even after what Janelle had done to him."

She took a seat and reached for the menu but looked at what I had in front of me. "That looks good," she said.

"You don't believe Will killed her for me?"

She shook her head. "You must have spoken with Kristy McDonald." She grimaced. "Don't listen to her. She's Janelle's sorority sister and best friend. She has a large blind spot where Janelle was concerned."

"And you're her adult best friend?"

Sydney chuckled and ordered what I had when the waitress came by.

"Janelle and I met at Murphy's. I worked there two years and left for something else. We did more than stay in touch. She was my best friend, and I was hers. We were very close."

"You knew what was going on with her recently?"

"Yes and no," she said. The waitress was quick with her order and placed her pie and tea on the table. Sydney took a bite of her pie before steeping the teabag in the hot water.

"How much do you know about it?" I asked and took a bite of my apple pie. It was quite good, and I hadn't realized how hungry I was until then.

"It's ironic that you'd be investigating. Janelle divorced Will, but the two of you coming together was hard for her. I'm surprised you agreed to do this."

I pulled out Janelle's note and handed it to her. Her eyes widened, her mouth dropped, her hands trembled as she read the note. "Oh," she said. "She knew she was in trouble."

"She did. What did she tell you about anything?" I asked.

"Not much really. It's just a lot of little things that keep adding up to a lot of bigger things. About two or three years ago, Janelle and Will went on a romantic vacation to the Caribbean. They were so excited. She went shopping for new clothes, hair done, the whole bit. But when they came back, things were weird. They were different. They sniped at each other; Janelle was hard on him. They started spending time apart. Neither one of them said what happened on that trip, but her friends always thought something happened on that trip."

And there it was, that magical time period. Three years ago. Did he forget about that trip? What could have happened in the Caribbean? Did Janelle meet someone? Is that when she started having affairs?

I waited until Sydney had taken another bite and swallowed.

"Did she tell you what happened in the Caribbean?" I asked.

Sydney shook her head. "No. She didn't want to talk about it. She posted early pictures on her social media and half way through the trip it stopped. She wouldn't say what happened."

"What differences did you notice?"

Sydney played with an apple on her plate. "That's the thing. Janelle was so organized, so prepared, so on top of everything. But after she came back from vacation, it was quite the opposite. She was forgetful, inconsistent and unreliable. That wasn't her. She was like that for a year or two. It was stressful and horrible for the two of them. I know they were fighting. And then, all of a sudden, after all of that, she asked Will for a divorce. We were all surprised. I spoke with Will on more than one occasion after the divorce, and he said it had been a long few years. They couldn't get pregnant and then she miscarried before the vacation. She started to have affairs after the trip. I was shocked that happened. She never shared that. I didn't even know about the fertility issues. I just thought she didn't want children. That's what she told me. For years."

Sydney looked up when a woman in a linen suit entered the restaurant. She waved her over. Hair was carefully coiffed, straight and shiny even in the heat and humidity of summer. She strolled over, confident and solemn. Sydney introduced me to Cathryn.

"Thanks for meeting with me," I said.

"Anything to find out what was going on with Janelle. It was so unlike her." She sat across from me, Sydney to my right.

Sydney caught her up.

"Any idea of who might have killed her?" Cathryn asked. She pulled Sydney's water toward herself and took a sip.

"I just started investigating. What I do know is she lost her job about four months ago. Lost her license six weeks ago. Did you know that?"

They both looked at me, confusion on their faces. "Had no idea."

"No clue. What happened?" Cathryn asked.

"She was sloppy at work and a misdiagnosis on her part led to a lawsuit against her and the therapy center."

"I can't believe she lost her license. She loved what we did," Sydney said.

"And she never told either of you about the lawsuit or her license?"

"No. She kept a lot close to her chest. She stopped telling us things maybe a year ago. We didn't see her much in the last year for sure," Sydney said.

"When you did see her, what was she like?"

"Guarded. Upset. At first, we thought it was the divorce, but I don't think that's what it was. She didn't talk about it much and when she did, she seemed relieved," Sydney said.

"We suggested she start dating, before the divorce was final, she reluctantly agreed. I think she regretted asking for the divorce, but she had cheated, and Will was ready to move on. You might want to speak to Neal Enders. They dated just before the divorce was finalized. He might know something we don't, though he wasn't around for long. Janelle wasn't into him."

I wrote his name on my pad of paper.

"You think it's all related to her murder?" Sydney asked.

"I do."

Cathryn raised her hand. I raised my eyebrows. "I didn't see Janelle much in the last year but there were two times that had me concerned. Both times I overheard some conversations that had no context until today. What she was discussing was concerning."

She took a sip of water. I waited with my pen above the paper.

"I don't know who she was on the phone with, but they were arguing. Janelle told this person that she was done. She was out and wanted nothing more to do with it. To stop calling her."

"She didn't explain after?"

Cathryn shook her head. "No. It was as if it never happened. The second call, I overheard, she was crying telling the person, a male voice, that she couldn't do that. She didn't want to hurt Will any longer. It was a bad idea, and she wouldn't do it."

"When were these calls?"

"The second call was about six weeks ago. I was at her house, she was upset, missing Will, but I think that was for my benefit. In the evening, I thought she was tired from a long day at work. The other call, about four months ago. Also, after work. If you need to find the caller."

"Thanks. I'll look into her phone records and see what I can find. Did you both know she was coming to Will's office harassing him, telling him she wanted him back?" They both looked surprised. "She came to my house too, told me he was her husband, and they'd be back together soon."

They glanced at each other and then to me. "We had no idea. What did she get herself into?" Cathryn asked.

"Based on what the lawsuit was about, I think it might have something to do with insurance fraud."

Again, they glanced at each other. "That's so not Janelle. She was always by the book. She took pride in her work and was well liked and successful," Sydney said. She glanced at her phone and pulled up a number passing it to me. It was Neal's number.

"Thanks. Both of you. I'm so sorry you lost your friend." I copied the number.

"Thanks for putting your feelings aside and doing right by her. I just wish she'd told us what was going on," Cathryn said.

"I'll keep you posted on how it's going."

"Thanks, Nikki. And tell Will if he needs anything, we'll be there for him," Cathryn added.

I watched them leave and paid for all the items before heading out.

Once in my car, I dialed Neal's number.

He answered immediately. I explained who I was and why I was calling.

"Oh. Okay. I'm sorry she was murdered. I'm not sure how I can help."

"I'm just looking to find out if you knew anything about what was going on with her before she died or overheard any phone calls or conversations with people about work."

He was silent for a moment. "I never heard anything. I'm sorry. I… it's just hard to believe she was murdered. I really liked her."

"Why did you break up with her?" While I was partially being nosy, it could be relevant, I told myself.

"It was all Janelle. She didn't want to go further in the relationship. She seemed a bit obsessed with her ex-husband. She said she wasn't feeling our relationship and wanted to end it."

I wondered if that's when she started coming around to see Will. But if she wasn't really that upset about the divorce, what changed?

"I'm sorry it ended badly."

"I knew she was going through something. I didn't know it would lead to murder. Everything between us was great at first, but things changed. And she was mean sometimes."

"Like how?"

"She made me feel awful about myself. I thought I was good looking enough, a good enough dresser. But I didn't make what Will made and didn't dress the way she liked and wasn't good enough looking for her. She started to compare me to Will."

"I'm very sorry about that. That must have sucked."

"It did. It was great at first. We had fun, great sex, but then…" he stopped talking.

"But then?"

"You and Will started dating. She became obsessed after that. She changed."

"Oh. I was under the impression her obsession might not have been real. That she wasn't really obsessed with him."

"It seemed real to me," he said quietly.

"I'm sure it was. I'm sorry. I'm trying to put the pieces together. A lot of people have different views about what was going on. You're confirming for me that someone else's perceptions might not be correct."

"I hope you find who killed her. But, wait."

"You remember something?"

"Yeah. Something odd. I saw her make out a to do list. She was looking to buy a gun. I thought that seemed odd for her, but she said something happened and the gun would make her feel safer."

"I suppose that makes sense seeing as something was going on with her. It must have scared her a lot. If you remember anything else, please contact me."

"Nikki, there's one more thing about that list. Your name was on it. It might have been a very good thing that she couldn't act on that." He silently hung up.

Based on the letter Janelle wrote, I don't think she was planning on killing me. I think she wanted to talk to me about what was going on sooner, and something, or someone, stopped her.

CHAPTER 5

No shouting, no crying, no name calling, no accusations. The kids who have spent the last three years huddled together, protecting each other from their relationship with their father, were now going through something. Could it have been the divorce and their almost non-existent relationship with their father that finally caught up with them or was it something else? As a mom, I wanted to step in and smooth it out, but I knew that wouldn't help any of us.

I had watched each of them leave this morning, one at a time, off to resume their summer activities. What had once been an easy summer spending it together, they were alone, and I was sad. It was well after 6:30 in the evening. The kids weren't home, and I was hyped up by what I had learned today.

After trying to study, I paced as I cleaned the kitchen, moved laundry from the washer to dryer and thought of Janelle's murder as I worked. Without a court order I couldn't access her phone records to verify what Cathryn had told me. I wanted to narrow down the phone calls, and if possible, discover who Janelle was talking to.

After folding the last of my shirts, I pulled up the latest email from Barry Mintz regarding the police investigation. Maybe I could find a legal way to get at Janelle's phone records, and I searched the evidence list. Luckily for me, Janelle's phone records had been listed among the thousands of documents already collected in the investigation. But there were no notes as to whether they discovered a clue or found a suspect.

I dialed Barry.

"Hi, Nikki. How are you?" he asked. He was typing as he spoke.

"I noticed in the list of evidence; the police have months and months of phone records. You think I can get me a copy?"

The typing stopped. "You have a theory?"

"I spoke with a friend of Janelle's who overheard two separate phone calls where Janelle was telling the other caller that she was done. That she wouldn't hurt Will anymore. I was hoping to narrow down who those calls were to."

Silence and then, "Hmmm. Do you have a date range?"

"Not exactly. But I thought with witness's help, I can

narrow it down. At least get a name."

"Let me see what I can get, and I'll send it as soon as I can. That's good work, Nikki. Thanks."

Barry took the news well, and I hoped he could get me what I needed before I had to make my way to the police station for it. All I could do now was wait.

***

At 9:00 p.m. I was back at the police department after a long day of interviewing potential suspects and witnesses. Susan, my favorite receptionist, was working the late shift and grimaced when I walked in.

I pulled out my email confirmation from Barry Mintz and placed it on the desktop.

She pulled it close, reviewed the confirmation. "Give me a moment." She walked away hurriedly, I felt as though I were interrupting terribly important work. There was nothing on her desk.

Barry had gotten permission for me to receive copies of the phone records collected over the last twelve months. I wish we could have gone back three years. I really wanted to know what happened during that magical time period.

I'd take what I could get.

"This is what the lawyer requested," Susan said when she returned twenty minutes later. While I waited, my thoughts turned to my kids, who arrived home one by one and headed to their rooms without speaking to each other. I barely got a hello. It was a quiet evening. Even Will was preoccupied with other things. I was actually looking forward to coming to the police station to get the phone records.

"This is what the lawyer requested," Susan said when she returned twenty minutes later. "I need you to sign this."

"Of course," I said and signed the receipt for the copies of the phone records. "Thank you." I handed back the form.

"I don't know who you know, but it's highly suspicious."

I raised my eyebrows. "The defendant, or person of interest is entitled to the evidence."

"And you think you can do better than the police?" Susan was clearly condescending, and I clearly didn't care.

"It doesn't matter. Mr. Mann's entitled to the evidence and what he does with it is up to him. Thanks for the copies."

I left before she could make any other snide comments. I was reflective as I headed home and grateful for the time being that Will was safe and the evidence might be in my bag.

***

There were a lot of calls in the last year.

I stared at the list as I thought of how I'd tackle the hundreds of calls and keep track of any patterns that might become clear.

"How's it going?" Will sat beside me and pulled up one month of phone calls.

"I've been reading and reviewing. I think I'll look for duplicate numbers first. And then do a reverse look up."

Will put the month of calls back on the bed and turned to face me. "You don't know how incredibly painful this is."

I could see it in his eyes. I knew. "I can stop. I can give this to Barry, tell him what needs to be done. Help him pinpoint the dates of those calls. I can stop."

He shook his head. "Don't stop. Do what you do. Find out who killed Janelle. Let her rest in peace."

"A little peace for you too."

I glanced at my phone. Jack was texting asking me if the kids were sleeping. None of them were answering his texts.

I let him know they were all sleeping and try them tomorrow. It was hard to be terse in a text, but he left that alone.

"You've got a lot on your plate," Will commented.

When didn't I? I didn't know any other way, and I supposed it was the life of a mom.

I shrugged.

"Things still need to get done. They still need a safe home; Janelle's murderer still needs to be found."

"And then there's me wishy washy about all this."

"Your divorce was finalized three months ago. Your ex-wife was murdered a week ago. There's a lot to unpack and to grieve. Give yourself a break."

"Have you started to give yourself a break?"

"Yeah. I have. Jack doesn't get to me anymore. Hearing about the baby or Amber doesn't send me in a panic. I only care that my kids are happy and healthy and that I'm moving forward. I'm glad I'm moving forward with you."

I reached for his hand.

"What can I do to help?"

I stared at the pile. It was after ten, and I was tired. I still had work in the morning, though I wouldn't be there for that long in the morning. There wasn't much to do.

"Nothing right now. I'll start this tomorrow afternoon when I get back from work. I'm going to sleep. It's been a long day."

***

Janelle made or received so many calls in a year. I'm guessing we all did but I never really paid attention to how many calls I received or answered because they were the simplest of communications with people outside of our homes.

I had gone through each month, each call, finding the duplicates by marking them with highlighters. Each bill was a bright rainbow of colors.

With each reverse look up, a clearer picture of Janelle's life became visible to me. She called her mom or her mom called her. There were calls to and from Cathryn and Sydney, even Kristy.

I could imagine the conversations with friends, calling her mom, reassuring her shc was okay, when she really wasn't. My heart hurt as I noted other calls to George Egan, short calls, mostly less than five minutes, most likely an order given or an update on the plan.

My phone buzzed.

Are we free tonight? Dad wants to take us to dinner, Jacob asked.

You're free. Have fun.

I sighed and returned to the list and the next reverse look up.

The next number I looked up belonged to a man named Marvin Gartner. What was interesting to me was the fact that the man's number was similar to another number Janelle had frequently called. I guessed the numbers were part of a block of numbers that belonged to a company. I looked up the similar number and learned it belonged to a company called Adams Medical.

Adams Medical?

I circled both numbers. I would look into those numbers more closely once I finished my list.

After finishing the reverse look up, I had a majority of the phone numbers assigned to an owner. I re-read the list and discovered I knew many of the owners. They were friends and family of Janelle's whom I had met over the years. While I had no evidence one way or another, I made the decision to not investigate friends and family. I doubted they had anything to do with what happened.

Whoever was left, I'd investigate.

Remembering what Cathryn had told me, I searched for calls from five to seven weeks ago and circled the ones that were unknown. In all, four of those numbers had been called several times. I'd have to contact Cathryn again to see if she could help me narrow the dates and times of the calls she overheard.

My phone buzzed again. Julia was complaining about Emily and Jacob. I told her to ignore them, assuming the kids were in the middle of a texting argument.

Putting the phone down, I returned to Janelle's phone bills. It was something, but not quite enough.

I rested against the back of the sofa, my legs underneath me. Closing my eyes, I let my mind wander and flip through the timeline. She lost her license, her job. Was there another source of income?

Did she work temporary jobs to make up for the loss of her income?

"Hi, Nikki. Anything new?" Barry asked.

"Yeah. Janelle lost her job, and I was wondering where she got funds to live. By any chance can you send me her bank statements?"

I was lucky with this one. That information was required as part of the divorce settlement and there was an abundance of bank statements going back five years.

"I've got five years for you. I'll send those on. Anything recent, I'll have to request from the police," Barry advised.

"Thanks, Barry. I can wait for those."

I had no choice even though those were the ones I wanted the most.

"No problem. Thanks for all of your work," he said before we said goodbye and hung up.

It never stopped feeling intrusive as I printed off each bank statement Barry sent. I was going into corners of Janelle's life that I felt as though I shouldn't be going, and yet I stared at the statements for the last three years.

At first glance, the statements didn't seem odd. Janelle had money. Regular paychecks for a decent paying job, keeping her expenses low. Alimony checks covering the rest, and I had expected that. But as I worked back through the months, something about the deposits made me tingle. Odd deposits in inconsistent amounts were deposited at varying times.

Another text, this time from Emily telling me that Jacob was hounding her about Marshall, swearing she didn't tell Marshall where she was going to be.

Mom, I didn't call Marshall. And now Jacob's pissed. Emily texted.

Ignore Jacob. Have fun with Lisa and Shelby.

I pushed my phone away and returned to the statements. I circled several deposits that were just under the $10,000 mark, interestingly as to prevent putting the deposit on the government's radar. Someone was clearly paying attention.

When I finally found the first payment, I noted, it had been made about a year after that three-year mark when everything started to fall apart.

Did it take twelve months to recruit her to the plan or to fully set it up?

I grouped the payments by medical companies or insurance companies until it looked as though there were five companies that were part of the scheme. Slowly, I worked my way through each company. While nothing seemed unusual at first glance, I looked for people, I looked up phone numbers, anything to tie the companies to the phone list. It all seemed innocuous until I found deposits from Adams Medical and one from Marvin Gartner.

Huh? Adams Medical, from the phone records.

What do you do, Adams Medical?

Successive texts from the kids began to blow up my phone. I couldn't keep track of who was pissed at who, and I finally sent them one final text.

I'm working. Please work it out on your own, I texted back.

"Ugh…" I said to myself as I returned to Adams Medical and reviewed their website.

The company seemed like a legitimate medical supplies seller. Was Janelle, as a speech therapist, using their products for her patients, and was she receiving a commission for doing that? If that were the case, the commission from Adams Medical seemed unusually high.

Was this related to her murder?

Maybe not but I did review the company on the Better Business Bureau website. I'm not sure why it surprised me that Adams Medical had been slapped with several complaints about insurance fraud, complaints of misdiagnoses, and another lawsuit a few years prior to the one involving Janelle. Not to mention, there were several fines, heavy fines, over the years.

Wouldn't Janelle and Murphy's Speech Therapy Center research this before partnering? Or were they chosen because of their nefarious activities? Or did they have something to do with recruiting Janelle?

In that moment, I knew I wasn't done with the speech therapy clinic. Either Debra knew more than she let on, or at least someone else at the center knew something.

More texts from the kids.

I'm working! We'll discuss later!

I shut off the ringer and pushed my phone away.

I clicked on the lawsuit I had just discovered. It was another family suing Janelle, George Egan and a second therapist named David Norman. Again, the complaint centered around a misdiagnosis with lasting effects. I noted the date. It was one year after the first payment from Adams Medical hit Janelle's bank account. And both events happened after the trip to the Caribbean. I looked at the results. The lawsuit was settled out of court and the final records were sealed.

She hadn't lost her job or her license as a result of the first lawsuit. But she had on the second lawsuit. Why? And why didn't Will tell me she had another lawsuit against her?

I called Will.

"Did you know Janelle was sued two years ago in another lawsuit against Murphy's?" I asked when he answered the phone.

"Uh. No. When was this?"

I explained the timeline. "She never told you?" I asked incredulously.

"No. She was stressed at work after the trip. It was part of the 'something was off,' but she never said anything. And you said it was settled out of court?"

"Yes."

"Murphy's must have paid for legal representation. I'm guessing they got as far as affidavits and discovery, and Murphy's knew they were in trouble. Damn. Why didn't she tell me?"

"She got into this scheme, insurance fraud, and she knew it was wrong. She couldn't tell you without letting you know about that."

"Do you have the second lawsuit?"

"I have it. I'll read through it and see what she did. You try to stay calm, and I'll see you tonight."

He was dejected when I hung up. A lawsuit was big news to hide from your spouse. I felt the same for him, and I realized I should have waited until he came home to tell him what I learned.

I looked through the lawsuit. It was similar to the most recent one. Janelle misdiagnosed an issue for the minor patient. He'd have lasting effects from the error. The phone records didn't go far enough back, but I compared the timing of the lawsuit to Janelle's bank statements. There was a considerable payoff prior to the lawsuit and a large payout after the lawsuit was settled.

I checked the recent lawsuit. The family claimed Janelle's boss, George Egan, approved the misdiagnosis. Also, the parents claimed that as part of the scheme to defraud the insurance company, Janelle submitted a more costly diagnosis and treatment for insurance. A treatment for the wrong diagnosis. Based on the lawsuits, George was clearly involved in the scheme. Did he bring Janelle in or did she bring him in?

There were no other lawsuits against Murphy's, Janelle or George.

I looked up David Norman. According to what I could find on him, on employment social media, he was working as a teacher in Southern Illinois. It was still summer break and after searching a bit on his site, I found a phone number and called him.

"Who are you again?" David asked after I introduced myself.

"Nikki Page. I'm investigating the death of Janelle Mann. I was hoping to ask you a few questions."

"I haven't seen Janelle in two years. I don't think I can help you," he said.

"I wanted to ask you about the lawsuit two years ago," I told him.

"Oh," he murmured. "I don't see how that's related."

"Janelle, George Egan, and Murphy's were sued this year, and the lawsuit hasn't been resolved yet. Janelle and George lost their jobs and their licenses. And now Janelle is dead. I want to know what happened that caused a client to sue the center and the three of you, two years ago."

He cleared his throat. "I don't see how it will help," he said again.

"She was committing insurance fraud. I suspect it was the same for the first lawsuit. What can you tell me about that?"

David hiccupped. "I didn't know about it. Not until the lawsuit was settled. I didn't participate in that."

"What do you know?" I said more harshly than I wanted.

"Listen. I had integrity. I worked hard for my clients. I did a good job. And then George overruled my analyses, made me change diagnoses, swapping cheaper solutions for more expensive ones. Just enough to make money, not enough to get caught. I couldn't take it. After the lawsuit was resolved, I quit, pulled up my life and moved away."

He was breathless as he explained his past.

"Did you know it was a planned and lucrative scheme before then?"

"I figured it out. I left before they dragged me into it fully."

"You didn't report it to the proper authorities?"

"No. I wanted out. I didn't want to get caught. It wasn't my idea, and it wasn't my choice. I wasn't going down because of them!" He was nearly shouting.

"I'm sorry. And I'm glad you got yourself away. The scheme's been going on ever since, and Janelle's dead because of it."

"I wasn't part of it. Not really. I wasn't paid, and I still suffered."

"You never met with anyone at Adams Medical? You never received funds?"

"Adams Medical was one of our vendors. I used them for my clients and called customer service as needed. But no, I never had clandestine meetings with anyone there."

"Did you know Marvin Gartner?"

"No. Who's that?"

"He works at Adams Medical. But if you never met with them about anything other than clients, that would make sense."

"I don't see how this helps?" David said.

"Do you remember ever seeing anyone odd come to Murphy's for a meeting or meeting any vendors that gave you bad vibes, or did you hear anything you shouldn't have heard?"

He was quiet on the phone.

"There were discussions. Lively discussions between George and Janelle. I walked in on one. They were discussing the client of the lawsuit. Even though I was being sued, they stopped talking, told me to leave it alone, they had it taken care of. I saw them meet with vendors, just the two of them. They seemed to meet outside of work. It was weird."

The two of them were into this plan together, sink or swim.

"If you think of anything else, can you call me? I'm looking for names, dates, times, anything to find out who could have killed Janelle."

"I'll think about it. If I have anything at home, I'll let you know. I hope you find what you're looking for."

CHAPTER 6

I ignored my buzzing phone as I worked through the investigative process. Janelle, George and David couldn't have operated in a vacuum. To work in a speech therapy clinic, you had the therapists who diagnosed the patient and coded the diagnosis and possibly sent to the manager for approval, before sending it to billing who would have sent it off to the insurance company and then to the patient for final payment.

According to David, he was forced to comply with the insurance fraud. Did I believe him? He left as a result of the first lawsuit, maybe his claim was true.

Debra, as far as I could tell, had been a therapist, promoted when George and Janelle were fired. Did she know and if she did, what did she know? She wasn't part of the lawsuit; I had just double checked.

I learned from Debra that Martha Hartman was in the billing department, and she would have touched each of the claims. I would suspect she understood what they were billing before she sent it to the insurance company. Did she know it was insurance fraud?

As far as I could tell, Martha Hartman's involvement, if there was any, hadn't been discovered or mentioned during discovery for either of the lawsuits.

I rubbed my eyes. They were blurry and itchy from so much computer time.

When the laundry room door opened, I turned, expecting one or all of the kids. Instead, it was Will trudging into the house, his tie untied, loosely hanging around his neck, his shirt wrinkled.

"Bad day?" I asked as he dropped his briefcase by the cabinet.

He shrugged. "A lot of catching up. I'm tired."

"There're leftovers I can heat up for you."

He sat at the table.

"What happened?" I asked him.

"You'll never believe this. The police left the office about an hour ago. They wanted to know what I knew about George Egan," he said.

My brain raced to my theory of where George Egan fell in the plan. "Why?"

"He's missing. His wife claimed he went on a business trip last week. But he hasn't been seen or heard from since. She did a little digging, and his birth certificate, passport, and banking information is gone, and she now knows there's a couple hundred thousand dollars missing in some accounts."

"And the police thought you might know something about it?"

He shrugged. "I knew the man, and my ex worked for him and was killed. So yes. They thought I might know something."

I kissed his cheek. "Let's get your dinner."

It was hot and late; I pulled out already made tuna and salad fixings as Will slumped on the kitchen chair.

"Can we assume George killed Janelle and ran?" Will asked when I put the salad in front of him.

"I wouldn't assume that. It could be he found out she died and is running to stay safe. He could've believed he was next. Did they say anything about what they found in his home? Letters, emails?"

"They did look. Found copies of the letters from Janelle to the insurance company." He looked at me. "Yes, my letterhead."

"He was also fired at the same time Janelle was. Lost his license too. What business meeting would he have gone to?" I asked.

Will shrugged. "That's a good question. I thought maybe he was dead and all of the clues made it look like he left?"

"I suppose that's a possibility. Do they still think you're involved?"

He shook his head, took a bite of the salad. "No. They don't. But they still think I know something."

"How well did you know George Egan?" I sat with my own salad. Mixed the dressing around the leafy greens.

"I knew him. But not well. It's possible he was the one who assigned Janelle the cases where there was fraud and he could have facilitated it."

"Cathryn told me she heard Janelle on the phone telling someone she wanted out. Supposedly, she was arguing with someone. It's possible she was telling George she wanted out."

"I don't buy that he killed her. It doesn't make sense. Why kill her if he needed her?"

"You're right, it doesn't make sense. I suspect Janelle was a warning to George and he ran," I said.

Will moved his food around his bowl. "I'm glad you're on the case. Thank you," he said quietly as he picked up a bite of food, put it to his mouth but didn't eat.

I sighed. "I love you." I stood and wrapped my arms around him from behind and kissed his cheek.

"I love you. I'm not sure I want to know how bad it really was."

"I can stop, and you can wait for the police report," I said.

He shook his head. "I trust you more than them. You'll do right by her."

"I'll try."

I had wolfed down my food and began to clean up the kitchen, expending the nervous energy swirling inside of me. Will ate each bite slowly as if contemplating it. I could tell George's disappearance made everything seem that much worse.

"Did you discover anything?" he asked and pushed his empty plate away.

"I called a speech therapist named David Norman. He was sued during the first lawsuit. He quit after the settlement. Claims he wasn't part of the plan but was forced by George to participate."

"I knew him. He seemed nice. I was surprised when he left Murphy's. Is he still working as a speech therapist?"

"No. A teacher. He quit everything after that. Have you ever heard of Marvin Gartner?"

He looked at me and shook his head. "I have no idea who that is."

"He works at Adams Medical. Janelle had many calls with him over the last few years. That company is one of a few that paid her."

"Any search results?"

"I've been up to my eyeballs in lawsuits and David Norman. I may stop by Adams Medical tomorrow and catch him at work." I cleared Will's empty bowl and finished cleaning up the dishes waiting for me.

Will sat at the table, absently looking out the bay window into the darkness. "It's been too much," he mumbled.

I reached for my computer and sat beside him.

"I made a decision," he said.

My heart raced when he said that. I was unsure of where he was going with his statement.

"Ok. What decision?"

He finally looked at me. "It's not what you think. Not really."

"What have you decided?" There were a lot of things it could be.

"I'm not ready to get married. I need time to get over Janelle's murder. I'm just not ready."

I breathed a sigh of relief. "Oh, thank goodness. I think it's too soon."

From outside, voices argued. Again. They grew louder the closer they got to the house. I looked at Will. "Something happened. They've been texting me all evening."

"I didn't tell him where we were!" Emily shouted the minute she walked into the house.

"The two of you are dumb!" Julia screeched. She ran from the group and headed upstairs, her feet pounding against the stairs, and then, she slammed her bedroom door.

"Ugh..." Emily said as she too ran off.

Jacob headed for the refrigerator and stared inside.

"Didn't eat when you were out?" I asked.

He didn't say anything as he dug around, finally finding the blueberries. He stood at the island popping them in his mouth.

I stared at him.

"What?" he asked.

"Nothing." I smiled because I couldn't find anything left to say. I returned to the table beside Will and opened my computer.

"Mom, what was that look for??"

I shrugged.

"Mom," he said with a bit of irritation in his voice.

"Now you know how I feel. I'm done with the fighting. Just go upstairs and get ready for bed."

Jacob reached around me and gave me a hug. "Sorry. She's just being unreasonable."

"I'm done with the name calling and judgment. Go on up."

"I'm sorry. Emily and I are trying, and we were out together when Marshall showed up at the outdoor concert. I got mad, she got mad."

"Is he following her?" Will asked.

"I can't say that for sure, except that he always seems to pop up where she is," Jacob said. He popped more blueberries in his mouth.

"Is she calling him and telling him where she's gonna be?" I asked. I stared at my open computer with the scant information on Marvin Gartner staring up at me. It was the typical fight with myself, mom versus paralegal. I returned my attention to Jacob.

"No, she's not. I'm thinking it's Lisa, or Shelby," Jacob said.

"Great friends they are then," I murmured as I stared at Marvin Gartner's work experience with Adams Medical as he had it on social media. I made a note on my pad beside the computer as Will calmed Jacob with soothing advice.

"Mom, are you even listening?" Jacob asked.

"Sorry, I've got a lot in my head and I'm trying to multitask. What do you need?"

"You need to talk to Emily and tell her to not trust those friends. And not to trust Marshall."

"I'm not telling her that." I looked at my unfinished research and closed down my computer. "Did you tell her this?"

"She won't listen to me."

"That's because you yell at her and call her names. Maybe if you tell her you're concerned about him and her friends plotting behind her back instead of accusing her, she might be open to hear what you say and think it through. I don't know Marshall well, but he sounds like an ass."

"Thank you," Jacob said and rolled his eyes.

"Sarcasm will cause your face to wrinkle," I said.

"I'm serious. I know I'm not wrong," Jacob said.

"I know, sweetie. You can't just blame her. You need to speak to her out of concern, not anger. And the two of you need to work out your differences. I can't do that for you."

I took my pile and headed upstairs. Knowing tomorrow, Marvin Gartner was my next stop.

CHAPTER 7

Several weeks ago, I first met Myles Landry. Well really, I met his alter ego, Lola Langston. She was in a caftan, all sparkly and flamboyant. I had been surprised at first, but on second and third glance, it turns out, Myles Landry/Lola Langston, was an amazing, beautiful, confident person. I had met Myles a second time when he came to the office and after meeting him the first time, I was a bit taken back. He was in his typical work wear: khaki pants, and a collared shirt. The drag performer was an all-around fascinating person, and I was amazed at how easily he moved from personality to personality; his confidence was what I aspired to.

Today, I walked into the restaurant, scanned the room and found Myles sitting at a booth by the window, wearing a t-shirt, jeans, and gym shoes. He spotted me and waved.

"Hi," I said as he stood and kissed my cheeks.

It was another look for him, one that he wore his confidence with ease. I wished I could be that sure of myself.

Since I lost my job and the subsequent part time work, I had lost some of that in myself which I supposed was why I saw that in Myles and seemed to pay undue attention to it.

"Oh, Nikki. Look at you." He spun me around. "You don't look as relaxed as I thought you'd be. Wedding planning or something else have you so stressed?" He pulled my chair out and I sat.

"Something else."

He grimaced, and I pulled up the menu.

"What happened to make my friend so visibly upset?" He looked at me inquisitively.

"A new case. But it's a little close to home." I took a sip from the water.

He put his hands on the table. "What happened?"

When I glanced at him, his blue eyes were penetrating. He seemed to really want to know what was up.

"My fiancé Will? His ex-wife was murdered."

He seemed genuinely surprised. "Oh, my. And you're investigating? That's good, the poor woman needs good help."

I nodded. "I haven't been hired, exactly. But Will wants me to investigate."

Myles took my hands. "But as you said, you're very close to this."

I explained Janelle's behavior over the last few weeks and the feeling that I was digging somewhere I shouldn't be.

"But Will trusts you to take care of her. I would think that would override your feelings. You're having doubts though."

The waitress came to take our orders. I already knew what I wanted.

When she left, I looked at my hands. "Janelle sent me a letter before she died, asking for my help. I feel as though I should keep at it."

"Then why are you debating it? Or do you like to wallow in the muck and overthink it?" He winked at me.

I chuckled. "I know. I tend to think and rethink and turn it over in my head. I can't help feeling like I'm intruding where I don't belong. It's making me anxious."

"You know, when you get hired by someone to dig into another person's life, are you going to be able to handle it, or is this because it's Will's ex?"

"I've known Janelle for almost twenty years. About three years ago, her behavior changed. Something happened and she started making bad choices that led her down a corrupt path. She was killed for what she did, or maybe didn't do, and I feel like I'm digging into her secrets and it's not my right to do so."

"Nikki. Janelle sent you a letter asking you for help because she knew she was in trouble. She possibly knew she was going to die. You're helping a woman with her dying wish."

I nodded again. He was right. "So, grow thicker skin and stop analyzing it to death?" I asked. Because the reality of the situation was, if I was going to do this for a living, I'd have to toughen up.

"Yes. Now. Would you like some wine, or is it too early in the day for you?"

We chatted happily over lunch and when our dessert arrived, I took a deep bite and moaned. Myles glanced at me and winked.

"I hear your landlord acquiesced and you finally got your clothing and other items back," I said when I pushed away my dessert plate. I couldn't resist the chocolate lava cake.

"Everything came back in okay condition as he threw all of the dresses into garbage bags, but other than that, yes. I have everything. Thank you for your work on the case."

"I didn't do much. He was clearly in the wrong."

Myles took the last bite of his brownie sundae. I watched him, and it must have caught him off guard. "What," he asked when he looked up.

"I feel as though you're my personal psychiatrist or something. I don't mean to put you in that position. You can, if you want to, use me the same way. I wouldn't mind, and it would be fair."

He laughed. "Consider me that friend. I really don't mind. I enjoy your company. Even if you're working through something right now," he said, his arms out wide.

"You're a nut. You know that."

"I aim to please."

It had been a delightful lunch with a funny man who, in the short time I've known him, helped me sort through the messiness of my life. I hoped that next time we met, there wouldn't be so much of it.

***

I thought of what Myles had said about a dying woman's last wish. After returning home and spending an unproductive hour on my PI studying, I returned to Janelle's investigation, regardless of how icky it made me feel to dissect her life.

But it was her life I couldn't get out of my head.

It occurred to me that her social media might unlock the secret of what happened three years ago. Granted, what happened on the internet was for show in most cases, a place where we create the life we wanted, not necessarily the life we had. But maybe I could glean something from what she posted.

Janelle's dying wish sat heavily in my mind as I scrolled through her pictures and posts from five years ago. She had been happy go lucky, you might say. Lovely pictures, sexy pictures, two good looking people so in love. My heart flickered as I watched Will's life roll out in front of me. I wasn't sure if it was jealously, envy, or anxiety, seeing him so happy with her, when at the same time, my life had been spinning out of control.

I kept scrolling forward throughout Janelle's life. Parties, weddings, vacations, more of the same. Had it been an illusion? I continued through her life until I reached that three-year mark.

More images of a happy couple, arms around each other, kissing, hanging out with friends, on vacation. On vacation. Still at the three-year mark, the pictures took on a different feel. Smiles not as wide, Janelle and Will no longer standing so close they could feel the heat of each other's skin. No hand holding or touching, no stolen looks.

Janelle and Will were in St. Thomas. The pictures were mostly outside, on a boat, or by a pool, and with another couple. I had never seen the couple before, and there they were on vacation with Will and Janelle, sharing meals, vacation outings. I wondered if they had met on vacation or had they known each other prior to going away.

I looked at Janelle's friend list and saw that the couple was Sebastian and Katrina Winston, and according to Janelle's page, they became friends on the trip?

Life was funny sometimes. You meet your closest friends, an instant connection in the oddest of places. Did that happen to Will and Janelle?

Who were Sebastian and Katrina Winston? I texted Will.

How did you find out about them, he asked.

Social media.

They're the start of everything bad.

Based on Will's curt answer, I think I had just found ground zero for everything changing. It could have been an affair between Janelle and Sebastian or Katrina for that matter. But how was that related to insurance fraud?

I did a simple search from my favorite databases and was surprised by the real lack of information on both Sebastian and Katrina Winston. The social media seemed to have been created weeks before the trip to St. Thomas and most of the information about them was only about a year old when Janelle and Will met them.

The red flags started immediately and the hairs on the back of my neck stood up. If they had new identities for that trip, who were they prior, and why did they change their identities? It could have been for many reasons, either they were running from someone and trying to hide, or they were con artists looking for their next score. Whatever the reasons for the identity change, I knew they were bad news.

I searched for lawsuits and properties and found a property downtown Chicago, an expensive address in a building on Lake Shore Drive.

But only Sebastian had that address. Were they even married? I wondered as I searched for Katrina.

She had about the same amount of data on her, also new, at least a year.

I did find a speech therapy license for Sebastian and an article on a website about a speech therapy convention in Chicago. It happened about six months prior to the trip to St. Thomas. Sebastian was a speaker at the event. I looked through his credentials but over the internet, couldn't verify what was true and what was made up. I knew sending a letter to the University of Illinois at Chicago asking for his information would be a data breach. I could only obtain that information with a search warrant, I printed what I could for my folders. But on careful inspection of the professional photo from the university, the picture didn't seem quite right. It wasn't exactly Sebastian.

So, Sebastian and Katrina Winston, who exactly were you?

CHAPTER 8

An hour in the office and most of the old files had been transferred to the clients' new lawyers. Extremely old files were sent to the shredding company to be destroyed. What was left were a small handful of clients that Samuel was keeping; easy work that he could do while retired.

Beyond that, office supplies, office equipment, and furniture would be picked up within a week.

I was pretty much done with the Samuel Ross era of my life. It had been very short.

I sat on the back porch sipping a tea, a letter written to the Palatine police department and to Barry Mintz, including my notes on the phone records and witness accounts in an envelope on the table beside me.

After a little digging, I discovered Janelle had been begging someone to be let out of the scheme in March and May. Both calls were made to a burner phone, so no name, no location, no viable clue.

But the police should know about the witness to the calls. There was a suspect somewhere out there.

When I wasn't sipping my now lukewarm tea, I watched the empty fire pit usually ablaze with flames during summer break. But lately, the kids were out, separated by their lengthy fight.

Without the laughter and happy chatting, the house felt lonely, and I was on edge.

I finished my tea and was ready to go inside when Will trudged up the deck. He had been working late and looked bushed.

He saw me, saw the empty mug, my computer held against my chest.

"Anything good?" he asked.

"I'm fine, thanks for asking. And you," I said.

He sighed. "Sorry. Long day. How was yours?"

"I found nothing except the day and time of Janelle's calls to whoever she was trying to end her participation in the insurance fraud."

"Burner phone?"

I nodded.

"And that's for the police?"

"And Barry."

He nodded. "Avers case. It's been a huge mess all week. Brothers are nitpicking each item, fighting over who deserves what. I'm trying to reign it in. It hasn't worked."

"Do you need any help on this?"

"No. You have your own work."

I had worked Avers client file when I worked for Will and for a bit after, but it became more complicated than I had time to give to it, so he transferred the work to his paralegal, my friend Wilma Haynes.

It looked like the client lawsuit was getting out of hand.

"Did you find Sebastian and Katrina Winston?" he asked when he sat at the picnic table.

"Those names were new. I couldn't find anything past a year old. Social media was about three months before St. Thomas."

"Of course they were. He claimed to be a speech therapist. I often wondered if it was truly a chance meeting," he said with his eyes closed.

"There's a good chance it wasn't. Sebastian was a guest speaker at a speech therapy conference about a year before you met him. Janelle could have met him there," I said.

"How did I not see this?"

"That he was completely lying about who he was? Why would you have known that?"

He opened his eyes and looked at me. "Something was off, and I knew it."

"Stop beating yourself up. You can't change what happened. I did what I could here and sent the police and Barry the phone records with my notes. In terms of Sebastian and Katrina, I have a lot of digging to do before I hand them this lead. I'll keep at it."

Will glanced at his phone. "Crap. Detective Clyde," he said.

"Hello Detective."

"Mr. Mann. I received an email from Mrs. Page. I don't think I like a lay person involving themselves in this investigation."

"My lawyer hired her to find Janelle's killer. Nikki's that good."

Resigned, he said, "Is Nikki there?"

He turned on the speaker. "She's here."

"I spoke with Cathryn Eichman. She heard two phone calls with persons unknown. Janelle was trying to get out of whatever she was into. I looked up the phone calls, and with Cathryn's help, I found the phone calls. Reverse look up showed the calls were to a burner phone. And no one is answering the number now."

For a moment, Detective Clyde was silent. "And you have the written witness statements?"

"Yes."

"Well good. Thank you for your information. But from now on, we'll handle the investigation. Please do not interfere."

He hung up and for him that was that.

"I guess I'm done," I said, a little burnt from that admonishment.

"I'd like you to stay safe and still look into it," Will said.

"I was reminded that my looking into this was the last wish of a dead woman. I'm not stopping."

Will took my hand, kissed the back of it. "Thank you for not listening to the detective."

***

The snipping started as soon as Emily and Jacob came home. Julia hid in her room, me in mine with my computer on my lap.

I had the St. Thomas trip that Janelle and Will took three years ago up on Facebook. I wanted his thoughts on what might have happened on that trip.

"The kids are at it," Will said when he came into the room carrying his tea and dinner.

"Unless they're physically killing each other, I thought I'd stay out of it." I pushed my computer aside.

"Find anything helpful?"

"I searched Janelle's social media, and I had a question about your vacation to St. Thomas?"

He looked at me with crinkled eyebrows and a downturned mouth. "Ok."

I turned the computer toward him. "By all accounts, she was very happy, excited to be going away. When she came back, she was sullen, cryptic, unhappy."

"I was excited to be going. I had no reason to think Janelle wasn't. We did have fun. The first few days were great. Even with Sebastian and Katrina. And then something changed. Like a switch. She didn't want to walk hand in hand along the beach, or have romantic dinners, or make love. She wouldn't tell me what happened. Just said she was not feeling great." He grimaced.

"Sebastian and Katrina? What were they like?"

"They were on their honeymoon, so they said. They weren't lovey dovey, hand holding types, and we were with them a lot. Dinners, hiking, the pool, a boat ride. They were enjoyable to be around. It was weird. After so many days with them, Janelle started to avoid them. She said there was something that made her nervous being around them. But then she disappeared one afternoon, and said she was going for a walk. I saw her talking to Sebastian. I didn't press her why. Figured they bumped into each other and were being friendly."

"When did she have her first affair?"

He cringed. "I don't know for sure. Months after that trip maybe. But then, she cheated on a serious boyfriend in college. She could have started long before St. Thomas. But her change seemed so gradual. Over a few months but very noticeable when you really think about it. But you're right, I think that was ground zero, so to speak."

I closed my computer. The voices from downstairs were getting louder. "I'm going to see what that's all about."

The closer I got downstairs, the more I realized that everything that had happened to me over the last ten months was probably responsible for this. Only time would tell if we'd get back to normal.

***

"Don't talk to me," Emily said as she stomped across the floor. Jacob followed, his lips in a tight grimace.

"He's seeing someone else. Why can't you see that."

I watched my eldest children, still arguing the same fight they've been having for the last week.

"I know that. Leave me alone." Emily caught my eye and reverted her gaze.

"What they hell are you two still fighting about?" I asked, coolness dripping in my voice.

"I'm going to bed," Emily said as she grabbed her purse and headed upstairs.

"She doesn't get it!" Jacob grumbled.

I stepped beside him. "Maybe she does, and you need to leave her alone," I suggested but Jacob glared.

"Seriously. It's like you being nice to dad all of a sudden."

"I'm nice to your dad for the sake of the three of you and that has nothing to do with this. Leave Emily alone. She's a big girl. She'll figure out whatever she needs to figure out."

I followed Emily upstairs and found her cuddled up in her bed, reading, streaming music, watching television. I wasn't sure how that was relaxing, but then, I wasn't nineteen.

I sat on her bed. If I surprised her, she didn't show it.

She took out one of her ear buds and turned off the television.

"What?" she asked.

"So, what's really going on?" I asked her.

"Marshall cheated, we broke up and now he's trying to get back together," she said simply.

"Are you encouraging him? Unknowingly or knowingly."

"Lisa and Shelby are telling him where I'll be. I'm not talking to them right now." She sounded sad not speaking to her friends. I agreed with her, especially if her best friends weren't respecting boundaries.

"Then why are you and Jacob fighting?"

Emily shrugged. "How's the investigation into Janelle's death?"

"Why are you fighting?"

She wrapped her arms around her bent legs and leaned on her knees. "He was worried about my relationship with

Marshall after the break up. He thought I was going to take him back, or be like you, nice to the ex." She grimaced and rolled her eyes.

"You know holding on to anger doesn't accomplish anything?"

She nodded. "I genuinely liked Marshall, but he cheated, and he wasn't very nice in the end. I learned from you, Mom, and you're right, being nice is for me, not him. But Lisa and Shelby won't drop it. I decided to spend less time with them."

I didn't understand why her friends were telling Emily's ex where she was going to be. Why would friends do that?

"Probably a good idea. I just wish you and Jacob would stop fighting. Especially since you are pretty much in agreement."

"I think he's taking out his feelings about you and dad on me. He's still angry you're not mad at Dad."

It was my turn to grimace. "I did it for the three of you. I make nice, and you have a better shot at a relationship with your dad."

I stood. "Try to work it out. At least stop fighting. And about Janelle's murder, I'm chipping away at the clues, but the police have warned me off."

"But you're ignoring that, right?"

"I'm ignoring it for now," I said.

"And Will wants you to," Emily said.

"I think I have a better shot interviewing those involved. But yes, Will asked and Janelle asked."

"Janelle asked?" She looked confused.

"Um. Long story. If you're okay, then I'll leave you to it." I stood and began to turn.

"When do you think you'll get married?"

"Winter break. There's too much emotional turmoil to do this before summer is out."

"It's got to be hard on Will with Janelle's murder. It'll be a fun winter break at least." Emily turned the television back on.

I took that as a dismissal and let her get back to her reading/tv/music time. When I reached my bedroom, I saw Jacob at her door and hoped their argument would be resolved soon.

CHAPTER 9

After an hour spent boxing the remaining folders and supplies for Samuel Ross, I was back home with a bunch of school supplies and some other desk items that Samuel offered me. I took what I thought the kids might use for school. The rest would be donated or sent along to other family members. It was early, still mid-morning when I arrived home to find a courier at my front door.

"Can I help you?" I asked the young adult, though I thought he could be as young as nineteen.

"Um, yeah. I'm looking for Nikki Page."

"Yes. What's this?"

He shrugged, handed me a tablet. "Sign there, please." I signed, and he handed me the envelope.

I grabbed a few dollars and handed it to him.

"Thanks," I managed to say.

He nodded and walked away.

"Who's that from?" Jacob asked when he opened the front door.

I glanced at the front of the envelope. It was addressed to me from a law firm I was unfamiliar with.

"It's from a law firm I don't know," I said and entered through the front door. I sat at the table and opened the thin 8x11 envelope.

Inside was a letter and a USB drive.

Dear Mrs. Page,

You are receiving this letter because you had yet to come to our office, Lewin, Lewin, and Oakes, to receive a package from our client, Janelle Mann. We knew that this would be a possibility that you may not have received instructions from her to speak with us. It's unfortunate that her fears of dying have come to pass.

Please review the enclosed information and contact us at your earliest convenience.

Mrs. Mann was certain you would be able to help her with her problem.

Sincerely,
Douglas Lewin, Esq.

"Um. Mom, what is that?" Jacob asked.

"Janelle left this with her lawyer for me to retrieve. She sent me a note before she died, asking to meet with me. She died before I received her request. I'm guessing she was going to tell me about this at that meeting." I held up the USB drive for Jacob to see.

"Mom, why'd Janelle send you all of this stuff? I thought she didn't like you."

"She needed help, though I'm not entirely sure why she didn't just send this first," I said as I stared at a single USB drive.

Jacob took the USB drive and walked to his computer, set up on the kitchen table.

"What did she get herself into?" Jacob inserted the drive, and the list of contents appeared on his screen. "There're five folders in here."

Letters, claim forms, emails, pictures, miscellaneous.

I stood over Jacob's shoulder. There were multiple folders in the letters folder. One was marked FBI, and Jacob clicked that one. There were hundreds of letters in the folder. "Sort oldest to newest and click the first letter, please." I instructed and watched as he pulled it up. The first letter from an FBI agent named Jackson Beale. "Oh," I said as I read through the first letter.

"What the hell," Jacob said as he read the letter alongside me. "She was working on a sting operation for the FBI?"

"Apparently. But look at the date. It was a little over a year ago." I re-read the letter. "Okay. According to this, she was working for them investigating her co-workers. That's strange," I said. "Pull up another. I don't understand why she lost her job and her license if she was working for the government in a sting operation."

Did they leave her hanging in the wind?

"Mom. If she was working for them, how did they let her die?"

I glanced at Jacob. "I don't know. You'd think they'd be watching the house or have a plan in place to protect her." I reached over Jacob's shoulder and clicked the next letter.

Still in the FBI folder, the next letter was also from Jackson Beale issuing instructions to Janelle. Her specific order this time was to work with Martha Hartman in billing and getting her take on a specific case. The FBI wanted to know what Martha knew.

The next three letters were copies of Janelle's progress reports to Jackson Beale, one of which explained how her conversation with Martha had gone and noting that George Egan had been directing Martha in her duties and threatened Martha with job termination if she didn't comply.

"What do you get from this?" Jacob asked.

"First, this confirms that Janelle and George Egan weren't the only two in the speech therapy center who were involved in this plan. The billing department had someone who knew what was going on and participated, though it looks like she may have been coerced. The other thing is, George Egan went missing so I can't ask him, and Jackson Beale has some explaining to do. Why didn't he protect Janelle?"

It seemed in the early days of Janelle's participation in the sting; she had been able to account for several of her co-workers and what their roles in the plan were. I noticed David wasn't among the list at first, but a final letter days before he quit, did point to him as one of the conspirators. After all of that, why hadn't the FBI gone after David and if they did, was there not enough to punish him for what he had done or did he walk because his testimony was that useful.

Jacob clicked out of the FBI letters and opened the folder labeled Adams. The first letter came from Adams Medical by way of Marvin Gartner, through the insurance side of the business. "This gives me more evidence against this guy, Marvin Gartner. Though I can't quite tell if he was her contact?"

Was this who Cathryn overheard Janelle speaking with on those two calls?

"I think it's time to speak with him," I said.

I continued through the letters. "Wow. She had gotten far into this case. She was so close to the top. That has to be why she was killed."

Another folder, this time emails from George Egan, Marvin Gartner, Benjamin Murphy, the owner of the speech therapy practice. According to another email, Janelle wasn't happy with what she had done and contacted the FBI as a whistleblower.

It all revolved around an operation to connect fraudulent claims to the office. Janelle had been responsible, but she had wanted out of the scheme. Jacob opened another folder with emails.

I glanced through several. "She saved copies of claim forms here, questionable items highlighted. Phone call notes. Try that folder."

In the picture folder, I noticed the sheer number of them in the one folder. I knew no one in the pictures until his familiar face smiled at me. There were pictures of Janelle with Will and another couple on a tropical island. Not close up pictures but surveillance pictures, long distance. When did Janelle start working in the plan? Was it after the trip or before? Who took these pictures and why? And were the pictures taken because of Sebastian and Katrina and Janelle?

My heart raced as I continued through the pictures, amazed at Janelle's case against these people.

"Mom, what do you think of all of this?"

"I think she was targeted for the plan. After years of fraudulent activity, she wanted out and couldn't get out. Based on what I saw in the FBI letter, she was the whistleblower. She went to the FBI," I said.

It should give Will some relief knowing Janelle was trying to make amends. Unfortunately, it wasn't soon enough. And her bizarre behavior over the last few months. What was that about?

I took over control of the computer for one last look at the documents. Janelle had highlighted signatures, diagnoses, and the approval signatures, either a billing rep, her boss, or the insurance company rep.

I had only looked through a fraction of documents, but I had one conclusion. I said, "It appears that it was only the three of them from the therapy center really in the insurance scam, and Martha was collateral damage. That doesn't make sense," I said almost to myself.

"What does that mean?" Jacob asked.

"Maybe it means she didn't have evidence against anyone else, or they weren't involved. It's just…"

I clicked and scrolled another few.

"It's just?"

"I can't believe that other supervisors or therapists didn't know what was going on."

Jacob took control of the screen and clicked the miscellaneous file. "Huh, what's this? It looks like a recording."

He clicked it. "Sebastian. I can't do this anymore. I'm out," Janelle whined on the recording. I glanced at Jacob; his eyes widened as if he was privileged to something secret. I reached over Jacob and clicked the recording off.

"I shouldn't get you involved." I tried to close the laptop. Jacob stopped me.

"I'm already involved in this. She came at you, at us. I can help. It's fascinating actually." He offered me a goofy grin.

I resisted the urge to rub his curly hair.

"There's PI client confidentiality," I said.

Jacob chuckled. "Seriously. Your client died before she hired you. I liked Janelle. Had a bit of a crush on her when I was younger. I'd like to help if I can."

I raised my eyebrows, mostly because he admitted what we all had known when he was younger.

"I know computers. Maybe I can get her computer," Jacob said.

"Fine." I clicked the recording and played it again.

"Sebastian. I can't do this anymore. I'm out," Janelle said.

"You're in too deep. You can't leave," said the low voice of Sebastian, at least that's who I assumed he was.

Will cleared his throat. I hadn't heard him enter. The clock said 12:15. I was surprised he was home, and Jacob hit pause. When I turned, Will was pale, his tie hanging around his neck.

"You're home. What's the occasion?" I asked as cheerfully as I could.

"The voice is Sebastian Winston," Will murmured.

I held out a chair for Will. "Sit. You don't look so good."

He shook his head. "I'm fine."

"Sit," I insisted.

Will stumbled to the chair.

"Why are you home?"

"More police questions. Asking about Janelle at work… what was she like there…did she enjoy her job. I needed a break, and thought I'd come home for lunch. Where did you get that recording?" he asked.

"I received a package from Janelle's lawyers this morning. Had we met before she died, I would have known to collect it from them."

I showed Will the letter. His law tightened.

"Play the rest," he said.

I held his hand as I restarted the recording.

"They're on to me. I'm going to lose everything. I need out. I'm done."

"They're not on to you. All those documents were legit. They don't know anything," he admonished.

"You're not listening. The government knows what we've

done. They're starting to come after me. I'm gonna lose everything because of you! I need out before it all crashes down around us."

"You mean crashes around you, sweetheart. There's nothing in there that ties me to you."

"Sebastian. You're not gonna help me?" Janelle pleaded.

"There's nothing to help. If the government figured it out, that's your fault. You're either in or they'll kill you. We're sending the Evans family. The kid has a palette issue that was surgically fixed. You know what to do."

"Sebastian, no. I won't do it."

"It's your funeral," Sebastian said and hung up.

I watched the blank screen. "Wow."

"If she was working with the FBI, why didn't they protect her?" Jacob asked.

Will stood and paced.

"I don't know. I'll give her contact a call, after I read through the emails and other things on this." This time, I minimized the screens and closed computer, taking the USB drive with me. I needed to think.

"Are you okay, Mom?"

I looked at Will. He looked as though he needed to hit something.

"She was alone. And crying out," Will said.

"We didn't know," I said.

He pushed the kitchen chair into the table, and it rattled and crashed to the floor.

"The FBI didn't protect her. You're right about that, Jacob. She was doing this to help them, and they let her down. I'd like her contact info. I'll call him." Will's eyes were wide, and for a moment, I was frightened by what I saw.

"No. You need to calm down and eat. I'll handle the call."

Reluctantly he stopped pacing.

"I'm gonna rethink how I go about this, though," I said.

Jacob touched my shoulder. "You're really smart."

I looked at him, confused by the comment.

"I mean it. You figured out what you wanted, and you went for it. You don't let this stuff get to you."

I laughed. "It gets to me. This is hard, because I knew her. Why don't you go upstairs and do whatever you're gonna do. I need to take care of Will."

Jacob let go of my shoulder and headed upstairs. I glanced at Will. He looked like a deer caught in the headlights, confused and scared. I needed to help fix this before I could fix anything else.

***

"Everything okay?" Will asked when I got back to the bedroom. He had showered, gained some color and looked a little less like he was going to punch the wall.

"For now," I said. I pulled up my computer and proceeded to pull up Adams Medical and Janelle's documents. I thought it was time to learn more about Marvin Gartner by meeting him.

"What's your next step," Will asked as I settled into the research.

"Adams Medical tomorrow. As far as I can tell it was Janelle, George, and Marvin. With George missing, Marvin's the last one standing. I'm not sure what he'll give me, but I need to find out what he knows. I'll call her FBI contact and find out what the hell happened. I also want to speak to Janelle's lawyer, Douglas Lewin. He might know more than what he sent me on her behalf."

"What do you have?"

It felt so much like he was trying to ignore an elephant in the room. Discussing what he had heard on the recording.

I pulled up Janelle's documents. "She sent me the questionable claims with those who had a hand in it. Martha Hartman, in billing, George and Janelle. I can't believe there aren't more employees involved, but that's what there is so far. I also see she was working with the FBI. It'll be contacting Jackson Beale from the FBI. I want to know why they didn't protect her."

I turned my computer to Will when I pulled up the pictures of the early surveillance. "Is this Sebastian?" I asked.

He looked at the picture, his jaw clinched. "Yeah. That's him. But why does it look like a surveillance picture?"

"Because they are. I think someone was watching Sebastian, Katrina, or even Janelle. I think she knew him before St. Thomas?"

He was thoughtful for a moment and then shook his head. "Nothing made me doubt that when we first met, but over the week…"

I looked at him. He seemed upset by that memory. "By the end of the trip, something was going on. Honestly, looking back and knowing what I know, I think he went after her romantically so he could go after her professionally. She didn't stand a chance; the manipulation was perfect."

I pulled up Sebastian Winston on social media. I found a nearly unused page. There was no woman with him anywhere in his photos. I checked other social media and concluded they most likely weren't married.

I couldn't find anything else to corroborate his marriage.

"Do you know if Sebastian and his wife were actually married?" I asked, breaking the silence. Will looked up from his work and frowned and then shrugged.

"I have no idea. She had an engagement ring, they both had wedding bands, but knowing what I know now, it could have been for show."

I continued to search for Sebastian, finally finding him working for American Speech Pathology Association, the same professional organization that Janelle worked for. "Why did he choose her?"

"What?" Will asked.

"Sebastian worked for the American Speech Pathology Association where Janelle was a member. You never heard of him before the trip?"

"I never had. If they knew each other, they didn't show it. They seemed mildly excited when they realized they worked in the same industry. Do you think he went after her on purpose?"

"Following her to St. Thomas seems a bit much, but if they weren't really married, then maybe they did. It doesn't seem probable though," I said.

"Odd maybe?"

"Odd definitely."

"If he were to plan an entire fraud scheme, he was in a great position to find a therapist with whom he could manipulate into it. Find them, blackmail them into working for him. Possibly seducing her into an affair and using it to blackmail her into the scheme. A fake marriage. It's a lot of planning but in this case, it seemed to work," I said.

"What if he has agents who talk to the therapist at their convention or through other means and glean things.

Someone finds out she was planning this trip, and they decide, it's a perfect set up. Send someone to St. Thomas, recruit her and make a lot of money on her," Will said excitedly.

"That seems farfetched."

"Maybe. But it feels like it's not a coincidence," Will said.

"I wonder if George sent Sebastian after Janelle," I murmured.

"Sebastian might be key," Will said.

"He just might be."

CHAPTER 10

Before calling anyone else, I wanted to get a handle on what Janelle had left for me. I followed the money.

Janelle's payments tracked back to Marvin Gartner. Based on business social media, Marvin Gartner was nothing more than a low-level customer service rep. Did he get the money from somewhere else and send payments to her? I couldn't imagine he was the mastermind, but then, maybe he cooked up the scheme and brought people in when he thought he could convince them to do it. How was it tied to Sebastian and Katrina?

I shuffled through the documents Janelle had wanted to show me. She clearly wanted me to know about Marvin Gartner, George Egan, Sebastian Winston and Katrina Winston.

Janelle hadn't thrown the clues in my face, I figured it was to hide her intentions should the USB drive get into the wrong hands, but I saw something in the examples of the fraudulent claim forms.

The claim forms Martha Hartman worked on had her initials all over the documents. Did she know about the insurance fraud, and did she know she was legally responsible?

So, was I looking at it correctly? Sebastian brought Janelle into the plan. She then brought in George Egan, and he forced David and Martha to comply. David got out before it blew up around him, and George was now missing.

And then there's Marvin Gartner who was sending Janelle her share of money for her work in the scheme.

Janelle's calls to Sebastian, her begging him to help her echoed in my mind. Did he recruit Marvin too or did Marvin recruit him?

"If Sebastian brought her into it, and wouldn't let her go, why'd he kill her?" I murmured to myself. I hadn't realized I wasn't alone.

"What, Mom?" Jacob asked.

I looked up. "Oh. Sorry. I didn't realize you were there. I'm talking to myself as I try to figure it out."

"You'd kill someone who was making you money if you discovered they had a secret," Jacob said.

"I'm thinking he'd kill someone she knew. Someone close to her. Parents, boyfriends, kids… Threaten her. Why kill a money maker?"

"Maybe she was killed as an example for someone else?" Jacob said.

My stomach roiled. That would mean Janelle was important enough to make a point but not important enough to keep alive.

If he was a recruiter, did he kill Janelle or did he hire someone to do it?

"What did she get herself into?" Jacob asked.

"Nothing good." I cleaned up my mess when I realized it was getting late.

"We're making dinner tonight," Jacob said.

"Oh. Okay. That's great. I'll be upstairs."

***

"They're quiet tonight," Will said when he entered the room. I had taken a shower to calm myself after reading through Janelle's documents. The more I read, the less I liked it.

I sat on my bed reviewing my private investigator information. My testing date was getting closer. I was starting to get nervous.

"I think they've started to work out their issues." No sooner had I said that than I heard a crash downstairs. I ran from the room and cautiously entered the kitchen. On the floor was my grandmother's heavy glass tray shattered in thousands of little pieces. I sucked in the air as my eyes swept the floor, hotdogs and hamburgers had been on that tray and were now scattered amongst the broken glass on the floor.

"Jules, get the vacuum cleaner please." I pulled out the garbage can, set it beside the mess. "All the food in the garbage. Be careful with the larger pieces of glass."

"Mom, we're so, so, sorry," Emily said.

"I know."

I took the vacuum from Julia and plugged it in.

"I'll buy you a new tray, Mom." Emily was near tears.

"No need. That was my grandma's tray. I have others." I bent over and picked up the larger pieces. Jacob joined me.

"Mom. I'm really sorry," Emily cried.

"Emily. Please don't worry about it. I have others. I promise it's okay." I touched her hand; she sucked in air and nodded.

I returned to picking up the pieces.

"Did you resolve your disagreement yet?" I asked. I scooped up hamburgers and the hotdog that had rolled under the dishwasher.

"We did until today."

"And what is this argument about?"

“Marshall’s friend Henry asked me out. Marshall is pissed, and Jacob thinks I should say no. I said yes. It’s one date!”

“With your ex-boyfriend’s friend. That could be trouble. Please think about the ramifications of that and why you’d even want to.” I turned to Jacob. “You leave her alone. Her life, her choices.”

When the mess was mostly clean, I wiped up the grease with soap and water. Emily took the rag from me and finished as Jacob followed after with the vacuum.

I pulled up the pizza joint on my phone and placed an online order. “Dinner will be here in forty minutes. The two of you, figure it out. Prolonging it is doing nothing for either of you, and it’s pissing me off.”

“Okay,” Jacob said without making eye contact.

Emily wrapped her arms around me in a hug. “Sorry,” she said.

“Stop apologizing about the tray. It might have been my grandma’s but it wasn’t anything special.”

“I mean about the fighting. You’re right about Henry.”

The doorbell rang. I was a bit confused, not expecting the pizza for a while.

“Expecting anyone?” I asked.

The kids all shook their heads and Will followed me to the door.

It was Detective Clyde.

“Detective Clyde. Is everything okay?” I asked.

“Yes, ma’am. There are some things I’d like to discuss. Can I come in?”

I motioned him inside.

“Thanks Mrs. Page, Mr. Mann.” He looked down the hallway, the kids were staring. “Is there someplace we can go in private?”

“They know what’s going on. Just go in here.” We sat around the dining room table and watched as the detective pulled out a folder and from there a document. It was a letter, on Will’s letterhead. He took it and read. His jaw clenched and tightened. He passed it to me when he finished.

Again, it was on the old letterhead but written nine months ago. An angry letter from Will to the FBI stating that Janelle Mann and George Egan were above board and within the law and to stop harassing his clients.

I noticed we were reading a copy, not the original. “Were Will’s fingerprints on the original?” I asked as I passed the letter back to him.

Detective Clyde fidgeted with the letter. “No. They weren’t.”

“What happened with the forensic computer expert who looked into Will’s computer?”

Again, more fidgeting as he put the document back in his bag. “We just received the results. None of the letters we discovered in Janelle's house were created on any of your computers. If they had been and deleted, they would have been found."

"So why are you here?" I asked.

"When did you find out about the letters?" Detective Clyde asked Will.

"When you showed them to me during my second interrogation," Will said angrily.

"She wasn't threatening you with these as blackmail?"

Will smiled. "You think she wrote these and blackmailed me? For what purpose?"

"To help her out of a jam," Detective Clyde said dryly.

"Did you check her computers? Did you find out if she wrote them?" Will said.

"She did. I can't believe you weren't angry at her for coming after you and your girlfriend. And I don't believe you didn't know about these letters."

"I never saw those letters before you showed them to me. Was I angry at Janelle for going after Nikki and coming to my office? Yes. I was angry."

"You know more than you're telling me."

Will stood and moved to the window, looking into the early evening.

"I know my ex-wife had affairs starting three years ago after a trip to St. Thomas. We think she was brought into this plan by a man named Sebastian Winston. I know she wanted out. She didn't tell these things to me. She asked Nikki to help her before she died. And Nikki has done more than you have to find out who killed Janelle. I don't know who did it. I didn't know what she was doing or how much trouble she was in. And yet, here you are again."

"Will has answered all your questions, I suggest, unless you have something new, you should leave," I said.

Detective Clyde nodded and didn't argue as he let himself out.

"What nerve, harassing you like that," I said.

"Be careful, Nikki. They could decide to charge you with obstruction. But thank you for getting rid of him."

I watched Detective Clyde leave the driveway and drive away and at the same time, our pizza delivery guy pulled into the driveway. "Dinner's here," I said as I returned to the kitchen for plates and napkins, not sure if I accomplished anything today and hoped the night would be a little quieter than it had been.

CHAPTER 11

The key to Janelle's townhome dug into my hip as I drove to her house. I hadn't been to the scene since she died. Actually, I had never been to her house, so I couldn't picture the last days of a desperate woman. I wanted the visual.

I sat outside on the driveway and looked at the cozy two-bedroom townhouse Janelle had purchased during the divorce. It might have been half the size of the house she and Will shared but it looked comfortable and welcoming.

The street was quiet. I wasn't surprised as most people were working, whether it was at home or at an office.

Will had gotten the key from her parents, and I used it to let myself in. Last time I entered a victim's home, I was caught by the police and arrested. This time, Will had gotten the keys from Janelle's parents, and I had permission from the next of kin to do what I needed to do.

As soon as I stepped inside, I could tell Janelle hadn't left her home this way. Items had been removed from drawers, closets, and seat cushions were dumped on the floor.

I knew the police had finished their search of the house, but her family hadn't been up for having the house cleaned and her items boxed up and taken out. It was still too raw and emotional for all of them. As I began to walk the house, I picked up decorative items and placed them where I thought they had gone. I fluffed pillows and tossed them in the sofa corners, folded blankets, and gently placed it on the armrest of the chair.

I looked on the shelves, in between pages of the books. As I worked my way through the mess, I searched for hiding locations, knelt beside the small fireplace and looked inside. I felt the flue, opened it but all I got for the effort was ash raining down on my arm.

"Awesome," I murmured and shook my arm and much of the ash off.

Pictures were askew, I assumed the police were looking for safes behind them or something hidden on the back of the picture. I picked up one of the paintings, an oil of a bouquet of sunflowers. If something had been there, it was gone now.

When the front room was tidy, I moved on to the kitchen, picking up food boxes, placing them back in the cabinets. I filled the dishwasher with the dirty dishes still in the sink and ran a nearly full dishwasher. I put away clean dishtowels, dishes, silverware, and glasses. I cleaned up food, looked inside the freezer for fake hiding compartments. Again, there was nothing unusual but had there been, the police probably already found it.

I moved on to the pile of papers near the extinct wall phone. I dialed *69 and let the phone ring to the last number Janelle had called from the phone. It rang several times until a voice message said, "Leave a message." I recognized the voice. Eerily, it sent me to Sebastian, and I disconnected the call.

Shit. Shit, he'll know whose phone that was from.

Anxious, but not ready to go, I continued through the pile of papers, also knowing that these had already been gone through and anything important was already taken.

Still, I straightened the pile and moved on to the upstairs floor and the bedrooms.

Janelle's small office had been cleaned out; computer, filing cabinet, whatever was inside the closet. The police took everything. The only thing left was an empty table used as a desk, office supplies in the open closet and the thick, burgundy stain where she had bled out. I shuddered as I stepped around it. My hands shook as I opened each filing cabinet drawer, glanced in the empty boxes in the closet. There was nothing left.

I bent down, looked under the desk, nothing was taped to the underside of the desktop or drawers.

Was I overthinking this search?

I moved on to Janelle's room, a soft, creamy, sophisticated woman's bedroom. Cream bedding, pink and blush highlights. I could see her under different circumstances coming up here to relax.

It wasn't a large room, and yet, it was roomy. The bed had been stripped, the drawers open and emptied. The entire contents of her closet appeared to be tossed across the bed.

I picked up a few items on her bed, a few blouses and hung them in the nearly empty closet. She had a whole organization system in there, and I looked through the drawers, the cabinet, and found nothing. I pulled down empty shoe boxes and started to clear up the shoes on the floor and placing them on the top shelf. I continued through the first pile and started on another. My phone rang, and I glanced at the clock. I had been here for an hour and hadn't found anything of consequence. I answered Will's call.

"Hi, babe," I said as I walked back into the bedroom.

"How's it going?"

"It was a mess. I straightened the downstairs; everything

is gone from her home office, and I started in the bedroom. There's not much here. Do you have any ideas?"

"Garage, maybe?"

"I'll try it next and head out. No police calls today?"

"None. I think they're finally done with me. You know, I almost forgot. Janelle often times had hidey holes around the house. Lifting up carpet corners, hiding things between the floor and carpet. I always thought it was weird, but she had done that our whole relationship."

"Hmmm. That means there can be something anywhere in the house."

"Try the master closet. She did that in our first condo."

I chuckled. "Thanks. I'll let you know if I find anything."

I walked through the bedroom with a new perspective looking for loose carpet and even under the dresser or bedside tables.

I entered the closet again, my eyes darting across the walls and the carpeted floor. I stopped on a bump in the corner of the closet.

Kneeling down I lifted the edge of the carpet, and it pulled up easily. I moved shoes that were still in the way and pulled again. It wasn't exactly as Will suggested. She hadn't hidden anything between the carpet and floor per se. Rather, she had a safe nestled between the joists. The lock was a combination lock with buttons, and I'd need the combination to enter.

First, I tried Janelle's birthday, then their anniversary date, finally trying Will's birthday. The safe popped open.

A simple notebook. I opened it, and it listed the names of the employees for Murphy Speech Therapy Center. Payments, I'm assuming by the amounts in a column. Lists of insurance companies, names of people at each company. Amounts of money peddled back to the insurance representatives.

I continued to clean out the safe and found several open letters from a man named James Coffee. Apparently, they were dating a year before she asked for a divorce. In the letter, he told her to not be scared, she was doing the right thing by helping the FBI with the insurance scam. He also went on in the letter telling her that bringing in Will was a brilliant plan to legitimize what they were doing. It wouldn't hurt if he was taken down too.

In another letter, James Coffee tells Janelle to not feel guilty about using Will. She's unhappy in the relationship and wants out. He reiterates Janelle's claim that Will was a bad husband and getting back at him was okay.

My stomach churned as I read what had been conspired between Janelle and her lover. Was her note to me just a lie to bring me into this, to help get her justice?

Could he be who Cathryn heard on the phone call? I thought I narrowed it down to Sebastian, but maybe I was wrong.

I put the letters aside and peered inside the surprisingly large safe. In a plastic bag I found bullets that looked like the .38 caliber bullet that killed her. There were prescription drugs for Janelle. I added them to the pile and reached in again. I found a large envelope lining the bottom of the safe and dumped the contents in my lap.

Mostly pictures and some letters. There were pictures of Janelle and her boss, more of her boss speaking with someone. I turned the picture over; confirming it was George Egan with a representative from the insurance company, trading envelopes. More pictures of the two men together. On the back of each picture were dates and times, not in Janelle's handwriting. I wondered if the FBI took these pictures and gave them to her to get her involved in helping them. But the letter she had sent me clearly made it seem she had gone to the FBI.

Were they the ones who were surveilling her in the pictures during the trip. Or were they looking into Sebastian and they caught Janelle in the process? Brought her into the investigation early?

Also in the envelope, a letter attached to a claim form in Janelle's handwriting with her initials. The letter from an insurance representative named Dennis Perkins, threatening Janelle, that if she went to the police, she would go down too.

The final picture I saw was her with James Coffee

according to the back notes. I read through the ledger and found Dennis Perkins and James Coffee. They were clearly part of the scheme.

After taking pictures of everything, I had found, I closed the safe, returned the carpet, replaced the shoes, and left the neatened house. I shoved the items in my bags and carried it from the house, locking the door behind me.

I drove away and headed to the police department with what I had found.

***

Armed with my notes and evidence, I waited in a conference room for Detective Clyde. He wasn't happy to see me.

"Mrs. Page. I thought I told you to leave us to do our jobs," he said condescending.

I opened the bag, tossed a pile on the table. "She asked me to help her. Before she died. I got a note from her and a legal letter from her lawyer giving me documents and her proof of illegal doings. I didn't know where else to go with this. Will told me she used to have hiding spots around the house. Weird places she'd hide things. I found all of that in a safe under the carpet in the closet. You're welcome."

I turned to leave.

"Mrs. Page, Mr. Mann could be charged with obstruction."

"He didn't think of it until I was cleaning up her house."

"Mrs. Page. I don't like amateurs messing in my case. I know you've had trouble before interfering with the police."

I walked to the door and turned the handle. "I helped solve those cases. I'll do the same if you don't drop Will from your list. She was part of an insurance fraud scheme to bilk insurance companies out of money. Lots of it. I suggest you read what I gave you. There are a lot of names."

He sat at the table and opened the folder, his jaw opening in surprise. "This was all in this safe?"

"Yes. Janelle's lawyer sent me a USB drive with even more information on it."

He motioned for me to sit. I moved to the table but stood and watched him peruse the pictures, reviewing the backs for notes. He glanced at the claim form then looked at the letters.

"She was helping the FBI," he said.

"Yes. She wanted out though. I haven't found who she was speaking with, but she told someone she was done," I reminded him.

"Someone wouldn't kill her for that. Maybe they found out she was working with the FBI."

"Or teaching someone else a lesson."

He nodded. "You know how to investigate. Can you send me what Janelle's lawyer sent you?"

I nodded. "I'm still sorting through the documents, but I'll send you what I have."

With pursed lips, he offered a slight nod. "Thank you for bringing it in."

I let myself out, pleased as punch.

CHAPTER 12

Adams Medical was housed in a nondescript office building with thin narrow windows along all four sides of the building.

It was larger than I suspected it would be, and the parking lot was very full. I parked my car at the furthest spot from the building and walked through the cars. No one was outside, the heat was hot and wet, and even the birds were silent.

The building was slick and new, and even smelled clean as I walked across white marbled floors. I walked past gold elevator doors, and walls covered in shiny, finely rubbed wooden panels.

Finding the receptionist's desk, I walked over and leaned against it as the receptionist continued speak on the phone. I tapped my fingers on the counter, but she continued to talk. When I knocked on top, she finally looked at me.

"Hang on a sec, I have someone waiting." She turned toward me. "Yeah."

I refrained from sighing or rolling my eyes even though I could tell from the conversation topic the call was personal. "I'm here to see Marvin Gartner," I said.

Her eyes grew wide, her hand shook, and she dropped the handset of the phone.

"He's not here," she said quietly.

"Do you know when he'll be back? It's important I speak with him."

"He's… he's… Mr. Gartner's not in. He's been out of town for two weeks. He was due back yesterday. No one's heard from him since he left."

"You know Marvin well?" I asked her.

She spoke into the phone. "I'll call you back." She returned her attention to me. "I know who he is, but I don't know much about him. We only chatted on his way to and from the elevators," she said.

"How do you know he was supposed to be back yesterday?" she asked.

She looked toward the elevators and the door to a hallway I assumed went to offices or other professional rooms.

"It's all over the office," she whispered.

"Why the secrecy?"

"Listen. He was kind to me, bringing me little gifts after vacations or on Mondays. He was a sweet, sweet man. But I'm worried," she murmured the final words.

"Was something wrong with Marvin before he left?" I asked. Her worry, and her quiet voice made me conscious of possible hiding spots for cameras or bugs. Something was clearly bothering her.

"He wasn't himself. He was secretive about where he was going. He didn't seem excited," her voice rose.

"Anything else you could tell me about him?"

"Like I said, I didn't know him well. He was so put together, a little frumpy and out of date, but really dressed smartly. Usually, he came in right at eight and left at five. He remembered names and stories. But recently, he was forgetful, coming in late, leaving early. He wouldn't let me pass calls or visitors up to see him unless he absolutely agreed to see them."

"Did he seem frightened?"

"I don't know. He seemed unaware. But he couldn't have. He had to have heard the rumors."

"What rumors?"

She looked around, to make sure we were still alone and fiddled with her phone. She motioned me closer to her.

"He was gonna be fired. Everyone knew it. He had to have known. He told his managers two weeks ago he was going away. For two weeks. Like he knew they couldn't fire him if he wasn't here."

"It wasn't a scheduled vacation, but an impromptu thing?"

She nodded.

"Do you know where he went?"

"He usually goes somewhere north in the summer and south in the winter. Which means he's probably at his rental property in northern Michigan, the upper peninsula. But he didn't tell me that. It's just a guess."

"Thanks for the information." I turned but stopped. When I looked back, the receptionist was staring at me.

"What does he do for the company?" I asked.

"He's an insurance claims handler."

"Insurance. Does he ever do anything for the medical supply side of the business?" I asked.

"We have two divisions, medical supply and insurance. The two are almost separate companies. Marvin adjusted and approved. He didn't handle medical supplies," she said, but didn't elaborate.

She was upset, and I felt it was a good time to leave. "Thanks for your help." I handed her a business card. "If you think of anything else, please contact me."

I left her alone, staring at her desktop. I'm sure I had hit a nerve.

I waited until I was in my car before calling Will.

"Hi, Nikki. How'd it go?"

"Marvin Gartner left on vacation two weeks ago. He was due back yesterday. No one's heard from him," I said.

"Oh," Will said.

"Oh, is right. The receptionist told me there were rumors he was gonna be fired. He left on an unscheduled vacation before they could."

"He knew what was coming," Will said.

"Did you know Adams Medical is not just medical supplies. A subsidiary of the company is insurance," I told him.

"Are you still there?"

"I'm in my car. I'm leaving now."

"Watch yourself on the way home."

That was my thought exactly.

But I couldn't shake that bad feeling, as I drove home from Adams Medical. Not that I was being followed because I knew I wasn't, but because first Janelle is murdered, then George Egan disappeared and now Marvin Gartner was missing. He left before he could be fired, but what if he hadn't left on his own?

As I watched the cars around me, I pulled into a restaurant parking lot and looked up Marvin Gartner's address. He lived near here, and I headed to his house.

I didn't have to wait long to find out what happened to Marvin Gartner.

When I arrived to his house, it appeared empty, curtains closed, and crime scene tape crossed the front door.

***

I pulled into the garage. Will's car was already inside. He was at the kitchen island eating an apple reading through a folder.

"No one told Adams Medical he was dead," I said to Will as I looked at the scant murder file for Marvin Gartner.

"He was killed before Janelle was killed and before George Egan disappeared. The day he called out for vacation, he was either running away because he knew someone was coming after him, or he was already dead, and the killer called him out for vacation."

"I'm guessing that was to keep anyone from looking for him," I said.

"And no one at Adams Medical thought to call him when he didn't return to work?" Will asked.

I shrugged. "I'd say they didn't like him, so they didn't miss him and forgot about him, but the receptionist knew and had a lot of information so that's probably not the case."

"Length of time since death won't hamper the investigation."

"But it does give the murderer time to prepare or go into hiding," I said.

I stared at the copy of the police file. His body had been discovered two days ago; a wellness check requested by his neighbor. "His neighbor knew something was wrong. Maybe it was the murderer who called the vacation in."

"So where will you go from here?" Will asked.

I pushed the pages together and stuck them in the folder. "James Coffee. Have you heard of him?"

"No. Who's he?"

"She was having an affair with him. I think he was the one who was trying to frame you in this."

"Oh."

"I'm sorry, Will. I know this sucks, but I need to find out what else he knows. If he could callously do that to you, I suspect he could harm her if she went against him."

"It's not that. I knew about the affairs; I didn't know she was planning on putting me in a legal quandary."

"I don't know if she wanted to. I think he was forcing her."

He put down his folder. "It doesn't help."

"I'm sorry," I said. I put my folder in my bag. There were two more people. "I also need to find Sebastian and Katrina Winston."

"Don't," Will said quickly.

"Why? He's next on the list. He's involved; we know that."

"He's the reason my marriage ended. He brought her into this. He got her killed or he killed her. I'm not putting you in that kind of danger."

"Then what? She wanted my help. You wanted my help."

"I can't put you in that kind of danger. Do your thing on the computer. But promise me you won't go after him, or Katrina, for that matter."

"You think he killed her?"

"I do."

I sighed. He knew Sebastian. I had to trust Will. But Sebastian was key. If he brought her in, got her killed he needed to pay for what he did. "Are you comfortable with me looking for Katrina? At least trying to find her?"

"I'm sorry, Nikki. After Janelle left, and I went through those emotions, I really moved on. With you. And I'll be damned if I let what she did, make me lose you too. I'm really happy. Happier than I think I was with Janelle even. Don't let her drag you into her mess. Not because Sebastian or Katrina."

I touched his cheeks with both hands and looked into his pained eyes. "I promise. I won't go looking for trouble. I can take the rest of this to Stan Marley. He can help me work through what I have and what's next."

Will looked at me, a slight smile. "That's right. You're starting with him soon."

I had received an email from him and the apprentice coordinator. It was all set as of today. "I got word today. I'll call Stan and see what he can do to help out."

Will reached over to kiss me. I wrapped my arms around him. It didn't ease the discomfort at knowing the one person who had the answers could destroy everything in my life if I wasn't careful.

I took that with me long after Will went to bed, and I lay beside him worried about the next step, wondering if I should take this to Stan Marley at all.

CHAPTER 13

I shuffled through my folders as Stan Marley let out a sigh.

"Will this be something we can work on?" I asked again. I had given Stan the detailed version of Janelle's murder case. His initial impression left me thinking it was a hard no, and I'd be relegated to background checks during my apprenticeship with him, at least for the time being. I was okay with that.

"It's not that the case doesn't intrigue me, because it does. It's like interfering with a police investigation before you've had official training isn't a good look, you know?" he asked.

"I suppose when you investigated Sabrina Crew, the police had already closed the case. I can live with that. I was hoping for some help though."

I was stuck. Will asked me to stay away from Sebastian and Katrina even though I believed they were key to Janelle's and Marvin's murders, and the reason George was missing. But I promised Will.

"The victim asked for your help before she was killed?" Stan asked.

"Yes."

He grumbled softly, and I thought I could hear him typing on his computer.

"Your fiancé wants you to investigate?"

"Correct. As long as I don't go after Sebastian or Katrina myself."

Again, his fingers clicked against his keyboard. I waited patiently for either his next question or his definite no on using Janelle's murder as part of my training. I thought that with Stan's help I might be able to have a crack at Sebastian and Katrina and solve Janelle's murder.

"I'll admit. You've been thorough, Nikki. Impressive, for sure. It would be a shame to not find justice for Janelle and the others."

He cleared his throat. This exercise between the two of us was wearing me down. Either yes or no, I thought to myself.

"And this Sebastian. Will thinks he's dangerous. I'm guessing that's why you want to tackle it in your training."

"That was my exact thought." I held my tongue. I didn't want to piss off the man who was holding my future PI career in his hands.

"The other problem is you're close to this case. You have to be careful and not let those emotions get in the way," Stan advised.

"I already know she wasn't perfect and did some very bad things. I think I can handle what I learn. I also don't think she deserved what happened to her. I plan on contacting her FBI handler about it."

"Okay. You're being levelheaded, but if you stop using your head, and I think you're being reckless or putting yourself or me in danger, I'll pull the plug."

"Understood." I reached for the folder and opened it again, feeling rejuvenated by his decision.

"By the way. We have ways to get at a subject and minimize danger," Stan said.

"A third party?"

"Yeah. Third party. He's discrete. I use him for recon often. He'll let us know what we're up against. If this dude is responsible for two deaths and a missing person, we approach it very carefully."

"Agreed."

"Saying all that, I'm in charge of this now. You'll do what's assigned and come to me for updates. Understand?"

"Yes sir," I said. Weirdly I felt relief having the control out of my hands. A little safer if I had to be honest. I was grateful Stan believed it was worth looking into.

"Now then. On to business. I have some background work for you. Keep good records on your time and any incurred expenses."

I chuckled. "No problem. Send it over and let me know what you're looking for. I'll get on it, right away."

"I'll get the works moving on Sebastian and Katrina Winston. You have enough to get us started."

"Thanks, Stan. For everything."

When I hung up, I opened my email and when his list came through, I read through his notes and pulled up the first name.

I set up my queries based on Stan's instructions and noted my time. The first query came in quickly but before I could dig in, I received a call.

"Hi, Will. What's up?" I said as I clicked a link to some information about my first background check.

"Janelle called Marvin Gartner. Her last two messages to him were on his answering machine. She begged him to stop the harassment."

"The police gave you the recording?"

"Yes. Nikki, it was awful."

Will was choking up. I could only imagine what she sounded like when she called Marvin. Though I wondered why she called him for help. It seemed like they were at the same level of the organization.

"She called Sebastian for help. Do you know when she called Marvin in relationship to that call?"

"The police used your timeline and based on that; they know Janelle called Sebastian about three days before she called Marvin."

I had been under the impression Sebastian was higher up in the organization and that she called him because he had sway. Was I that wrong?

"Does that mean Marvin had more pull to get her out of there?"

"Janelle told Marvin she was being followed and specifically asked him to call off the dogs. His response was cold when he advised her to rethink leaving. The more he denied her request, the more anxious and upset she became. Crying. She finally promised she'd stay on if he'd stop the men from following her. She was terrified. I've been sick about it ever since the police played it for me."

"Even promising to stay, he couldn't help her."

"No, he couldn't, or he chose not to. I'm betting he chose to let her hang out there to give himself time to prepare to leave."

"I talked to Stan about the case. He agreed to investigate and guide me through it. And the good news is, he has means to get at Sebastian with low danger to me or to him. He'll work on that, and I'll work on the first background checks for him."

"Ah, that's great. I'm glad he'll take the case, so to speak."

Will sounded awful. I wasn't sure I'd be able to help him through this.

"Are you gonna be, okay?"

"I will be, eventually. Thanks for everything. I love you."

"I love you."

I finished with Will and felt a little unsettled as I worked on the background checks. It was simple work as I printed off and marked up the sheets, looking for what Stan had requested. I set up what would become a final report, filling it in with the initial scant data I had found. Eventually, it would fill out and give Stan the picture he was after. For now, it was not much of anything.

When I had gotten as far as I could on the initial queries, I made my notes for my next background checks and set up the queries.

While they ran, I returned to the list of people involved in the scam.

I started with Jackson Beale. I looked him up online and prepared for a conversation with him. Really what I wanted to know was how he let this happen.

There wasn't much to find, and I understood why the FBI wouldn't want the information publicly available. I returned to the letters from Jackson to Janelle, found his phone number and dialed.

It rang and rang and finally, "Jackson Beale."

"Hi Agent Beale. This is Nikki Page. I'm a PI apprentice working on the Janelle Mann murder investigation. I have some questions for you regarding Janelle's time working as an informant for you."

He didn't answer, nor did he hang up.

"Mr. Beale?"

"I can't discuss an ongoing case," he said.

"Does that mean the FBI is investigating how they let Janelle die?"

"We, I didn't let her die. I tried to get her out when she knew they were watching her. I was … too late."

"Did she tell you who she thought was behind it?" I asked.

"I can't tell you that," he said. He was clearly upset and shattered by what had happened to Janelle.

"You're looking into Sebastian Winston?"

"Don't go after him. He's dangerous."

I took that as a yes. "I'm not going after him. She called him for help. She called Marvin Gartner for help. Marvin's dead."

"I know," Jackson said quietly. "I'm sorry, Mrs. Page. I can't help you. But please understand, I feel awful about what happened to Janelle and Marvin. I will live with the mistakes I made for the rest of my life."

"George Egan is missing."

"I know," he said.

"How did it happen?" I asked.

"I watched her. We had eyes on all the players. I don't know how it happened."

He hung up. I didn't hear the click, but I felt it.

I must've been on the right track where the investigation was concerned. Sebastian Winston was key.

I had other work and checked on the queries, reviewed the new information and added it to the report in bits and pieces. I printed off pages, circled new information and queried more.

When my computer churned out the next batch of queries, I returned to Janelle and her cohorts, knowing they were involved on some level.

I couldn't get the information I needed: bank statements, phone records, personal and for each company.

Would Detective Benson Clyde just give them to me?

I didn't think so but called him anyway.

"Mrs. Page. How can I help you?" He sounded as if I had interrupted something extremely important.

"Have you checked Martha Hartmann's and Teddi Hanson's bank statements and phone records? I can't believe the billing department and receptionist at Murphy's didn't know what was going on," I said.

"We have pulled those items for the entire staff," Clyde said, resigned in my attempt to get information.

"And?"

"Mrs. Page. This is highly irregular. I can't just give you that information."

"But we can work together. I can help. I have helped," I pleaded, undignified and all.

He sighed audibly, for my benefit and shuffled papers.

"Ms. Hanson is the receptionist," he began to read. "Her role was to book new clients. Not all, but many were vetted by Marvin Gartner and sent over. She coded the files for Janelle and George's approval. They then went on to billing and Martha Hartman. We have payments to both women from Adams Medical and several other medical operations. We've been using the phone records you reviewed and sent me; we were able to match up several of the names, though we don't see Sebastian or Katrina Winston as ever having contacted any of the other staff. That relationship went through Janelle only."

"It looks like Janelle may have been targeted by Sebastian, and she brought the entire staff into the plan." I grimaced. Why and how could she have done that?

"I'm sorry. I know you had a relationship with her prior to this, but it does look like that yes."

"What other medical centers, hospitals or insurance companies were a part of this?" I asked.

"We were able to find additional medical centers, doctors and the like that weren't in Janelle's purview. Not only were there payments from Adams Medical but there were payments from Robert Hubble, MD, a drug company called Leeway Drug and Therapy Center. All the deposits were around $5,000. For Ms. Hanson and Ms. Hartman, the payments were between $3000 and $5000."

"So, they had less of a stake in the plan. Janelle was bringing in $10k."

"I agree. Janelle was deeper into this. But she was also trying to bring it down. I did speak with Jackson Beale. They screwed up, and she's dead. Marvin's dead. And with George missing, there's a bit of a lull in what else we've been able to find," Clyde advised.

"What about David Norman? He worked there and quit because of it."

"We did check into his accounts because of the prior lawsuit. He was paid what Janelle was paid."

"He must have had the level of a risk or importance as Janelle. Is he working with you?"

"He's in a lot of trouble, so yes, he's assisting. I can send you what we have."

"Is there anything I can do to lift some of the burden?"

"I was going to look into Leeway and Robert Hubble, MD. If you'd like to try your hand at that, I can work on George

Egan and Sebastian Winston. They're out there somewhere, and I suspect even if Janelle brought George into this, he was higher up on the food chain, and he's hiding. Probably from Sebastian."

"Thanks Detective. I appreciate you sharing with me."

"I suspect if I didn't, you'd find this out anyway. I might as well share what I have. Besides, I have a letter from Stan Marley, and he requested that I assist you in any legal way I can as you are working on this through him."

Ah. So that's why Clyde was so helpful.

"Thanks again. I'll send you anything new I find."

It was easier than I expected it to be. When my next queries were done, I added new information to my background checks and continued through Stan's very long list. When I had a good breaking point, I switched to Leeway and Robert Hubble, MD.

The information was more of the same. The lawsuits, the complaints of fraudulent claims. But there was one that caught my eye. Patient, Marshall Pointer. I knew that name, the boy who was harassing my daughter, otherwise known as her ex-boyfriend. His parents had sued Robert Hubble, MD, and several members of his staff for misdiagnosing a problem with his speech delay. He wasn't speaking until he was nearly five and in kindergarten. He was sent to Janelle and Murphy's after the lawsuit concluded, and the Pointer family won an undisclosed amount of money.

Huh?

So, Janelle was connected to Robert Hubble, indirectly. I had wondered why in all of her documents she hadn't had anything from Dr. Hubble or Leeway. I wondered if that meant they worked specifically with one group of organizations. But why? Wouldn't that set off red flags?

I wondered if Marshall remembered his time with Janelle Mann and his speech therapy work.

CHAPTER 14

It took all I had to ask Emily for Marshall's phone number. He was confused when I asked him to meet me. But he was on time as I sat on the bench overlooking Lake Zurich. The promenade was empty today.

"Mrs. Page," Marshall said as he sat beside me.

"It's a nice day out today. Thanks for meeting with me."

"No prob. I'm just confused by how I can help, and what's it got to do with me?" he said.

"Your name came up in an investigation but not as a suspect or anything like that. I was curious about what you remember about Janelle Mann and your experience with speech therapy."

He was silent as he leaned back against the bench. A motorboat flew in front of our view and was gone in an instant.

"I don't remember much. Just there was an old guy who worked with me and then a pretty woman. Janey, I think."

He looked at his hands and picked at loose skin around his nail.

"Janelle," I corrected him.

I pulled up a picture from Janelle's social media and showed him.

He smiled. "Yeah. Her. I wasn't speaking so good when I was five. She came in and made it better."

Not so well, but I kept my mouth shut. I held my phone in my lap.

"I found a lawsuit. Your parents sued the doctor, and you were then sent to Janelle. Do you remember anything about it at all?"

"Not much. I heard Jane… Janelle was killed a few weeks ago. How that stuff when I was a kids, help with this? It was a long time ago, Mrs. Page."

"You speak well, so I'm assuming her therapy was good."

"Yeah. I guess."

I pulled up a picture of George and showed Marshall and then swiped to Marvin. "Either of these men look familiar?"

He stared at the screen and went back and forth between both men.

"Nope. Sorry."

I pulled up Sebastian and showed him. Marshall bit his lip as though he was thinking. He shook his head. "Nope. Who is he?"

"Person of interest. And what about him?" On a whim, I pulled up the picture of Janelle's boyfriend, Neal Enders. He was also on her social media site. I wasn't sure why I was doing this, but it seemed like something to do because of the connection between Janelle and Dr. Hubbard.

"Um. Yeah. I've seen him. Not recently, but I remember him. Who's he?"

"Neal Enders," I said.

"Neal Enders? Hmm. Sorry, I don't know the name," Marshall said thoughtfully.

"You really think you've seen him before?" I asked.

"Yeah. I recognize him. But I don't know why. I kinda think of cookies when I see his face, but I don't know why. Sorry, Mrs. Page."

I handed him one last picture. It was a James Coffee. Again, he had no idea who he was.

"Thanks Marshall. I appreciate your time." I stood and pocketed my phone.

Marshall stood beside me. He was a good seven inches taller than me, and I looked up to catch his gaze.

"One last thing."

He looked at me with a bit of fear in his eyes. "Mrs. Page?"

"Leave Emily alone. Tell her so called friends, Sidney and Lisa, to stop calling you with where she'll be. You broke up with her, so leave her alone," I said, and I walked to the street, looked both ways and jogged my way to the parking lot. I got into my car, and Marshall, still confused and fearful, watched me leave.

***

Murphy's center was quiet for a Thursday afternoon. I expected that even without Janelle and George, and now Marvin, business would be slowing down as they were the bulk of the insurance scam.

I entered the one-story office building and crossed the lobby to the front entrance. Teddi Hanson watched me walk in; her eyes widened as I entered the reception area.

"You need to leave. We're very short staffed, and you've already caused enough damage with your questions," she said with a higher voice than normal. I understood the stress of the situation, but I didn't bring this on them. They just happened to get caught.

I walked to her reception desk; she picked up the phone. "I'm calling security. You need to leave."

I reached over the high desk top and easily took the phone away from her. "You're not calling security. You need to answer some questions, and I promise I'll leave. It's in your best interest to talk to me now," I said.

Stan didn't know the developments yet; I had only promised not to go after Sebastian. I wanted to know if there was something to Neal Enders.

Teddi's hands shook, and that was all that I needed to know about her participation. "What was your role in the insurance fraud?"

She shook her head.

"I know you took money from Adams Medical and Dr. Hubble. What was your role?" I asked harsher than I had wanted.

She moved to take the phone receiver; I took the entire phone.

"Based on what I've already learned, Sebastian Winston sent people here. Did he call you to let you know who was coming in? Did you have to mark the intake forms so everyone else knew the patient would be scammed? Was that your role?"

Tears started to flow from Teddi's eyes. "I didn't want to do this. Janelle told me I had to. At first, I didn't know why. But by the time I found out what it was all for, it was too late. Once they paid me..."

"So you took the appointments, marked the forms so the rest of the staff knew the patient was part of the scam. Did you do anything else?"

Teddi's hands clenched tightly, her face turned a pale, ghostly white. She wiped the tears from her cheeks leaving makep streaks across her face.

"Courier," she said.

"You ran money, records, what?"

"All of it. Sebastian had me pick up things and return things. I ran money, claim forms, and medical equipment. I picked it up and delivered it." She hiccupped and sniffled.

"Nothing else?"

Teddi shook her head.

"Is Martha in?"

"No."

"You sure about that?"

"I've told you what I know. You need to go," she whispered loudly.

I took out my phone and showed her a picture of James Coffee. She didn't react. "You've never seen him?"

"No."

I switched to Sebastian. Again, there was no recognition. "You sure?"

"I've never seen him."

"Okay. One last picture." I showed her Neal Enders.

"Oh." She nodded in recognition. "I've seen him. He's a friend of Janelle's. He came in several times a few years ago. We thought it was odd. She was still married to Will, but he came in, and they seemed to like each other."

"Thanks. Is Martha in?"

"I shouldn't."

"Janelle is dead, and George is missing. Your whole center is in trouble. I suggest you all start preparing how you're going to help the police. Because they're narrowing in on everyone here. So, I'll ask again. Where is Martha?"

I followed Teddi's instructions and walked through a door down a narrow hallway. At the end of the hallway, I knocked on the door.

"Yeah?" a voice said.

I opened the doors and found who I assumed was Martha Hartman at her desk. It was immaculately clean, several desk organizers holding folders, papers, desk supplies. Martha, a young woman, slightly overweight, stared at me with wide eyes. Acne scars pocked her face. She was dressed in nice slacks and a blouse that was only slightly tight. She quickly looked away.

"I'm busy," she said and opened up a folder. She didn't fool me; it was empty.

"So, you're Martha," I said. Whatever system she used to keep organized was well hidden behind cabinets and drawers.

"You have nothing on me."

"I'm Nikki Page. I'm investigating Janelle's murder, and yes, I do have evidence against you, as do the police. Well actually, Janelle collected the evidence. I assume you all knew by whatever codes Teddi put on the intake forms, who would be part of the scam, and you billed accordingly. To Marvin Gartner, possibly."

"We... how... how?" she hung her head. "How did you know that?"

"Janelle was working with the FBI before she died. She sent me what I needed. I'm trying to figure out who killed her and Marvin. I have my thoughts. Possibly George, possibly Sebastian. What do you know about that?"

"Marvin's dead too?"

"He was found dead this week. We think he was preparing to get out of town but misjudged how much time he had." I sat in the chair across from her.

She sat in her desk chair, her hands tightly wound around each other. She was squeezing so tightly, her knuckles were white.

"I can't. We know we're in trouble. But we promised Mr. Murphy we'd stay on until he could hire replacements." She looked away. "Oh, I can't take this anymore," she screeched.

"Then tell me who killed them. Who's responsible for this plan?"

"I don't know. Janelle had me do this. I don't know what it all means." She glanced at the lamp on her desk. "I wish you would leave us alone. The police have already been here. You need to leave."

I pulled up the pictures on my phone, but as it turned out Martha hadn't been there long enough to know Neal Enders or anyone else for that matter. Even the picture of Sebastian went unrecognized.

I pulled out my business card and slid it to her and walked out the door. I left a shaking Martha in her office and walked to Teddi's desk. She was alone in the waiting room. Teddi lowered her gaze as I left the building.

As soon as I exited the building, I ran for my car and locked myself inside. I dialed my phone.

"Special Agent, Jackson Beale," he said.

"Not only didn't you protect Janelle, George Egan, or Marvin Gartner, Teddi Hanson and Martha Hartman are left exposed. They're terrified of something," I said quickly, and my voice was nearly unrecognizable to me it was so high and stressed.

I held my phone tightly as I scanned the parking lot for any car that made my stomach roil.

"Mrs. Page? Are you still at Murphy's?"

"Yes. Martha Hartman and Teddi Hanson are terrified. You need to put them in hiding. Do something to protect them."

"We are doing something. We've got eyes on Sebastian Winston though his supposed wife Katrina hasn't been located," he said.

"Do something to protect them!" I shouted at him. I started my car.

“We are. We have people at the office and at their homes. Do not tell me what to do again,” he said and the line went dead.

I pulled out of the parking spot and out of the lot on my way home. I wondered if the FBI was watching me now. My eyes scanned the roads, the sidewalks, the cars around me. My hands shook as I drove home. I breathed a sigh of relief and dialed Stan.

“I just got back from Murphy’s,” I said, my lungs struggling to calm.

I stared outside onto my street. I couldn’t believe I was seeing another strange car in front of the neighbor’s house. Again.

“How did it go?”

“I talked to the receptionist Teddi Hanson and the billing woman, Martha Hartman. They’re frightened of someone. Most likely Sebastian, but they didn’t recognize a picture of him. Has your third party started recon?”

“Yes. If those women are that frightened, you need to back off. Stay away from anyone that has to do with the case.”

“I agree. I’ll continue with the background checks. Though there’s a beige four door car watching my house.”

I heard a deep sigh through the phone. “Send me a picture of the license plate, and I’ll tell you who it belongs to.”

“Will do. But there’s one weird thing. I was researching a Dr. Robert Hubble. He paid the two women at Murphy’s.

About fifteen years ago, he was sued and his patient ended up working with Janelle. That patient is my daughter's ex-boyfriend, Marshall Pointer."

"Not a coincidence?" he asked.

"I would have thought so, but I spoke with him and just for giggles had him look at some pictures of the players. He recognized a man Janelle cheated on her husband with about three years ago. A Neal Enders. It was fifteen years ago, and yet, he recognized him but doesn't remember where. I did show Teddi and Martha. Teddi recognized him as a friend of Janelle's. I think Neal and Janelle have known each other for a very long time, and I'm not sure what it means."

"And your interest was?"

"The link between Janelle and Dr. Hubble. She had no interactions with him in the fraud scheme, while he paid Teddi and Martha. Janelle and the doctor's paths crossed years ago and because of a lawsuit."

"And this young man remembers the boyfriend from years ago. And you're wondering if it's something or not."

"Pretty much."

"What's your gut telling you?"

"If there wasn't a connection between the patient, doctor, and therapist from back then to now, I never would have gone down this road."

"I suggest you finish up the list I gave you, and then you look into Neal Enders. It's definitely a weird connection that could mean something."

"Thanks, Stan. I'll send you the license plate."

I hung up with Stan, shot the picture of the license plate and sent it off. I grabbed my computer and set up the queries, pulling up the next layer of information Stan requested. As that ran, I paced from the kitchen to the den and back again, and when the doorbell rang, I froze.

Whoever it was knocked on the door then rang the bell again. I walked to the dining room window, close to the front door, opened it and said, "What do you want?"

A man in a black suit was confused by the disembodied voice. "Where are you?" he asked.

"That doesn't matter. Who are you and what do you want?"

My phone buzzed; the car belonged to the Drug Enforcement Agency.

"Mrs. Page. I assume that's you. I'd like to speak with you," the man said pleasantly.

"Again, tell me who you are and what you want."

He found my location, turned and stared at the bushes in front of the window where I stood. I backed into the hallway, not in direct contact of the window.

He held his badge to the window. I slowly made my way back to the window, took a picture of his badge and walked back to the hallway where I sent the picture to Stan. "What do you want?" I asked for the third time.

"I need to talk to you about Janelle Mann's murder. I found your name attached to a whole mess of evidence with the Palatine police department."

"What do you want to know? From what I can tell you're the DEA, and I haven't stumbled on a drug ring."

"You've stumbled on Sebastian Winston and Katrina Lowell though."

"I'm guessing they're not married."

"Can you let me in. I really would like to speak with you."

"No. How do you think I can help you?" I glanced at my phone. Nothing from Stan.

"How much do you know about Sebastian?"

"My fiancé met him three years ago on a vacation with his ex-wife. It was the beginning of the end of their marriage. I know he is somehow part of the insurance scam. I'm not sure how high up in the organization he actually is or how much pull he has. I don't know anything else."

My phone buzzed.

He's legit, and that's his picture, Stan said.

I opened the door and stared at the man named Lester Roland in his suit, standing in my garden, amongst the bushes.

"I don't know anything else. You can go."

"You got confirmation I'm for real."

"Yes."

"Have you made contact with Sebastian?"

"No. I haven't, and I won't be any time soon," I said confidently.

"Because you are in that file in the chain of evidence, he could find you too."

I felt my knees grow weak, and I held onto the front door frame. "What do you want from me?"

"To keep me in the loop. We're stationed in several locations looking for him. We think we have a location for him, and we'll be placing a man in this area to watch you. The FBI was watching Janelle, and she got away long enough to end up dead. Same with Marvin and we can only assume George is dead. We're assisting and will be watching you to make sure you stay safe."

"Why is the DEA involved in the insurance scam?"

This couldn't be happening again. I knew I needed to get the kids out of here. But would someone go after them to get to me?

"Sebastian is a jack of all trades. He connects people. He has a large network and is currently working insurance fraud. Part of that is the distribution of pain medications. He does that through clinics such as the speech therapy clinic and smaller medical centers. He thinks it keeps him off the radar. It really doesn't." Lester Roland grimaced.

"How much danger am I in?"

"We don't have any chatter to indicate you're in danger, but we do have someone watching you."

"How large is his organization?"

"Large enough we noticed. The DEA is working with the FBI, and we're working with local police."

"Is he the top guy?"

"We think he's in recruitment. Medical professionals, insurance players, and patients. Katrina is his partner in this, but we haven't been able to locate her."

I wondered if the murderer killed Katrina too.

"Thanks for the warning. Are you the first one watching me?"

"I'll be here today and have someone watching tonight. Promise me you'll keep me posted." He pulled out a card and slipped it in the flower pot beside the door.

He stepped backward, nearly tumbling over the bush behind him. Once he righted himself, he walked the stone path to the driveway and down to the street, climbing back inside his car, watching me.

I went back inside, locked the door behind me as I decided the best way to approach what to do with my kids and wondered if becoming a PI was the best option for my life.

CHAPTER 15

I didn't care how obvious I was as I stared at the DEA agent still parked outside. Lester Roland watched me and periodically, his partner would take a stroll around the neighborhood checking out the back yard and the neighbors' yards. It was a bit nerve wracking and yet, my gut told me I wouldn't be seeing Sebastian any time soon. Katrina either. They had nothing to gain from coming after me.

Was I telling myself that to make me feel better? Possibly. I'd relax a bit more once the kids came home. But my brain switched to where I could take them, that would be safer than here.

Will's townhome? Mom and Dad's?

I rubbed my temples and took another turn around the downstairs as I tried to settle myself. I took three turns around the rooms. I stopped at the front window and noticed Roland Lester's partner return to the car.

I couldn't help watch the car as the inhabitants watched me.

I don't know how long I had been there when my phone buzzed. The kids for now, were coming home for dinner.

Maybe that was enough to kick me into gear. I returned to the kitchen and my computer. I think I had a plan should I need one, and I forced myself to concentrate on the work that needed to be done. A murderer was still walking free, and Janelle deserved my attention.

I looked at my recent notes, particularly my phone call with Neal Enders. The connections between the various parties had me troubled.

During the conversation, Neal sounded mild mannered and genuinely upset by Janelle's murder as much as he seemed saddened by the end of his relationship with Janelle.

But then maybe he was glad the relationship was over. It sounded as though Janelle had compared Neal unfavorably to Will. I would have thought he would have been angry at her, but he didn't seem to hate her or hold any ill will toward her. If that wasn't an odd piece of information, Neal was connected to Janelle, who was connected through Marshall Pointer, by the way of Dr. Hubble, and Dr. Hubble was also a part of the insurance scam.

Were those connections purely coincidence, or was there something there?

My gut told me because of Dr. Hubble and Janelle's roles in the scam, there was something to investigate.

Before speaking with Neal again, I pulled him up online. I found pictures of him and Janelle on her social media profile pages. In the pictures, Janelle and Neal appeared happy, at least in the beginning. But as time moved on, I could see the crack in the exterior. But then Neal admitted the relationship didn't last long.

Knowing they dated after that magic three-year mark, I went farther back in Janelle's timeline. I found Neal on her friend list and searched his pictures, finally finding what I was looking for. Janelle and Neal together in romantic pictures that went all the way back to college.

Much younger, much happier, dopey in love. I remembered those days. That early love, when you're just learning about yourself. I thought of Krista McDonald and what she had said about Janelle cheating on a boyfriend in college.

I saved a picture of Janelle and Neal and sent it to her.

Did Janelle cheat on him in college?

I wasn't expecting a response. I was surprised when it came.

Yes. How did you find out?

Long story. But thank you for the confirmation.

I scrolled through the pictures of Janelle and Neal on his social media page. I couldn't help but think their relationship in college meant more to Neal than it had to Janelle, since I hadn't found the older pictures from college on her page. How did they reconnect after she asked for a divorce? Did he reach out? Did she contact him?

Did it matter?

Probably not, unless Neal was involved in the insurance scam, which from what Janelle had saved, there was nothing to say that Neal was involved.

So why was I so focused on Neal Enders? It came down to the connection to Robert Hubble all those years ago and the connection he had to Murphy's Speech Therapy Center.

It was a connection.

And it sat at the pit of my stomach telling me I needed clarity.

I dialed Neal and thought of all of the connections as I waited for him to answer.

"Hello?" he asked, confusion in his voice.

"Hi, Neal. It's Nikki Page again. I had something I needed to ask you. I hope this isn't a bad time."

"No. No. It's fine. How can I help you? Have you found Janelle's killer?" he asked.

"I haven't. I wish I was closer. But the thing about an

investigation is, it's all about finding connections. To people, to places, to little pieces of information that add up to a bigger picture. And when you find all the connections, usually you can find the answer," I said.

"Oh. Okay. So how does this involve me?" he asked, his voice a little nervous.

Did I hit a nerve?

"I have a list of people who are somehow related to the investigation. They are known as persons of interest. They know something or had a role in the illegal activities. And you look at the persons of interest to see how their relationship with the murder victim started and ended to discover if they have a role in the victim's death. Does that make sense so far?"

"Am I a person of interest?" he asked earnestly.

"Yes and no. You're more of a witness since you have something to add about Janelle's behavior leading up to her death."

"I would hate to think you were looking at me for Janelle's murder. I really cared about her," he said earnestly.

"I could tell that when I talked to you earlier. It must have hurt when she started to treat you badly."

"It did. We weren't right for each other. I've moved on."

Did you really? I thought to myself.

"As I was telling you about connections, I have a list of persons of interest who have a role in the events leading to her death. One is a doctor who is certainly part of the insurance scam. As I investigated him, I found a connection between him and Janelle about fifteen years ago. That gets my brain rolling with possibilities," I said.

"That's something. Really. You think this doctor was responsible for her death?"

"I don't have any evidence about that, but I do think he was a cog in the plan. Possibly in her death. So, I looked at their connection. A young patient that the doctor worked with and misdiagnosed. The result sent the patient to Janelle for treatment. Do you see how weird that connection is?"

"Yeah. Yeah. That is weird. The doc and Janelle worked together years ago. A misdiagnosis. Something bad. Yeah. That's interesting. So, you are looking at this doctor then?"

"I am looking at the doctor. But I have one other connection that I found odd when I was looking into that patient case. I know the patient. Weirdly enough, he's friends with my daughter. I would have just called it a coincidence if it hadn't been for the doctor. Doing my due diligence, I happened to ask the patient if he knew any of the players involved in the case, both suspects and persons of interest. That's why I'm calling you."

"The patient recognized me," he said matter of factly.

"This would have been about fifteen years ago. And before you deny it, I found pictures of you and Janelle on social media. Some pictures back as far as college," I said.

He laughed, and even without knowing him, it sounded nervous. "So, you caught me. I've known Janelle for years. I fell in love with her in college. We were young, it didn't last. We reconnected about fifteen years ago after a mutual friend's wedding, but she was married so it didn't go anywhere. I met up with her again while she was divorcing. We had history and were comfortable together, but dating her during her divorce was hard. She was still struggling with the divorce and was a bit mean. I forgive her for that and will always love her."

"Even after she cheated on you in college?"

He coughed, cleared his throat. "How did you find that out?" he said angrily.

"Connections. I interview people who knew her and her situation. I put together the connections."

He didn't say anything.

"She died two weeks ago. When was the last time you saw her?"

"I haven't seen her in months. I didn't kill her. Happy now?" he said.

The line went dead. I clearly hit a nerve.

***

"Connections." Stan laughed when I told him about my

conversation with Neal Enders and what led to it. "That's good. I'll have ta' remember that."

It was after midnight, and the inside of the car was dark. We were sitting in his basic black sedan in a high-end neighborhood, outside a house that had ties to Sebastian Winston. It was my first official stake out, and we were there merely to take in the neighborhood and get a lay of the land.

Sebastian obviously had money from some source.

"The kids are safe?" Stan asked.

I looked through the binoculars at the house with ties to Sebastian. It was a small mansion, Italian in style, large bushes around the perimeter of a large lot, I assumed was over an acre.

"Yeah. Will's there. The DEA is outside, and they take turns walking around the house," I said.

Nothing was happening at the house and hadn't happened in the hour we'd been sitting there. I wasn't expecting anything, but I was hoping for more.

"Still no movement," I said, though we figured the house was empty as the windows were dark.

"What have we learned?"

I caught a whiff of the car as I thought of what I had learned. The car smelled like old fried food and stale air. Even with the windows cracked, it wasn't the most pleasant smell, but I loved sitting here in the car taking this all in.

"Well, I know that we're in a wealthy area. Which means, if he rents, he has money, if he bought the property, he has money. What he does pulls in big money," I said as I rattled off the first impression.

"And?"

I knew he'd want more.

"Well, there are thick hedges around the property line for privacy. And if you look carefully, it looks like a fence on the other side bushes. The address is hidden from sight. It's not on the house or on the mailbox. There are no streetlights in this neighborhood. That makes it difficult to see anything around the house. Privacy is a huge issue."

I continued to scan the bushes, the mailbox, the part of the house that rose above the bushes. Beside the gate to the fence that crossed the driveway, appeared to be a thick lamppost and a small metal door. "I see something."

I handed Stan the binoculars. "Right side, in the stucco post."

He took his time as he looked through the binoculars, humming as he viewed the house.

"Yeah. Yeah. That looks like a door with a hinge. You stay here," Stan said as he pointed with each word.

I knew better than to disobey my current boss. I nodded as he handed me the binoculars and snuck out of his car toward the house.

He opened the small metal door and peered inside. When he turned back to me, he held up an envelope, I could see it plainly through the binoculars.

I watched Stan look both ways and run back to the car.

"So?" I asked when he closed the door.

Stan shrugged and carefully lifted the flap of the envelope. He pulled out a small note.

"Camera," he ordered and held the note out for me.

I shot a picture with my phone before I could even process what we were looking at. When I took several for good measure, he placed the note back into the envelope and ran it back to the box.

I stared at the picture when he ran back to the car and slammed the door shut.

"Anything?" he asked.

"It's code, and I'm not seeing anything obvious." I showed him the screen.

After staring at the phone for several minutes, he said, "I got someone who can look at this. Randy Titan." He pulled out his phone and showed me the number. I texted the picture to Randy.

"Who's Randy?" I asked when I sent the text.

"He's a code guy. Been in the military as a code breaker. He does this for fun," Stan said. He took the binoculars and looked at the house starting at the second story and moving his way down.

He looked down the street and back again. "I'm not seeing anything. But I'd sure like to see who comes out and gets that code," Stan said as he trained the binoculars on the metal box.

"We've been here a little over an hour and haven't seen anyone. I'm guessing it was put in there in the dark when there's likely not gonna be anyone outside."

"Which means?" Stan asked as he watched.

"The code went in the box before today. It could have been out there for a long time or as soon as last night, late."

"I tend to agree with that. If it's important, it should be picked up sooner rather than later. You got time?"

"I was expecting a long night," I said and texted Will with my ETA or lack of it.

"Hand me a cake, will ya'?"

I opened up the snack cakes and handed him the package. Without taking his eyes from the house, he reached in and pulled out one, taking a large bite.

"I wonder if this is a report or orders," I said as I looked at the pictures again. Nothing in the codes made sense. I couldn't even see a pattern.

Beside me, Stan tensed, and I looked up. It was after midnight by quite a bit, 12:42 to be exact, and I could see a shadow cross the yard. I ducked low but gave myself enough room to see over the dash and watched intently as the shadow crossed back and stopped at the post where the box was.

Within seconds, the shadow crossed again until it disappeared inside the foliage and probably inside the house.

"A report," Stan said. He looked down the street once again before leaving the car. I watched as he ran across the street and opened the metal door. He came jogging back to the car let himself in and closed the door.

"We missed the messenger, but someone in the house took that note," Stan said. He turned on the car. "I don't think we'll see anything else for the night. Any questions?"

"You're contact is sure Sebastian owns this house?"

"A holding company owned by him owns the house, but yes. This is one of his properties."

"How often do you want to come out here and watch the place or are we done for now?"

"We got lucky tonight. I suggest we don't come back." He turned toward me. "I mean it. Don't come back."

"I won't. I'm sufficiently scared enough of him to not do that."

"Okay then. Let's head home. See what Randy has to say about that note."

Stan started the car and drove us away from Sebastian and his secrets.

CHAPTER 16

It was my first real stake out, and we hadn't gotten much, in regard to Sebastian. At least not until Randy, whoever he was, told us what the note meant, if he could even break the code.

I walked into the house at 2 a.m. hyped up from the night. Needing to calm down for sleep, I put a pot of water on to boil and prepared chamomile tea to help me sleep.

"Hey," Will said as he shuffled into the kitchen. I had woken him from sleep. His hair was mussed, and he shielded his eyes from the low light over the island. "How did it go?"

I shrugged and poured the water when the kettle whistled.

"I'm not sure. We found a hidden mailbox with a coded note inside. We're waiting for a code breaker to see if he can crack it. Otherwise, I'm not sure we accomplished anything."

“The joys of stake outs.” He sat beside me. “Just to let you know, the DEA has been and is still out there. They’ve been walking the neighborhood. So far, it’s been quiet.”

I nodded. “How were the kids?”

“Quiet. I’m not sure if they’ve worked out their issues or they’re staying away from each other for the time being.”

“Thanks for keeping things in order here.”

He grabbed my free hand. “Anytime.” He pulled a file closer to him. “So, nothing new tonight. Do you have plans for the next step?”

Inside the folder were notes and bits and pieces of what she had sent. Things I wanted to look into further. Janelle had only gotten me so far; I needed to take what she left me and find the meaning. I seemed to be stuck on the weird coincidences which told me nothing about who killed her. Suppositions meant nothing at trial.

“Well, I have a link I can’t shake. It’s Dr. Robert Hubble, who treated Marshall Pointer. When the doctor was sued, Janelle treated Marshall and that connection leads to Neal Enders. All in all, it could be completely unrelated, but yet that single moment in the past is somehow connected to a murder today. I just can’t find the relationship in the present day, because it appears Janelle and Dr. Hubble aren’t connected now.”

“But because they were involved with the same patient

back then, you think they were mostly likely connected now," Will said.

Will opened the folder.

"She knew the doctor was involved in the insurance scam. She has him listed on these claim forms. Why isn't that enough to prove a connection?"

"There's nothing that shows they worked together on a case. She could have just copied the documents to prove he was involved, but just not with her."

"But she has the connection to Murphy's. That's enough," Will said. "They could have kept the connection a secret because of the past. Plausible deniability. You just happened to stumble across the past."

"Just happened to…"

I took the claim form with Dr. Hubble's name and notes on it and took a sip of tea. Why was I so obsessed with this connection? Was Janelle going to out Dr. Hubble, and he killed her to stop it? There was nothing to prove who killed Janelle in this line of investigation. Was I wasting my time?

"You should rest. I know you're not tired, but come to bed." He kissed my cheek.

"Give me a few minutes. There's something I want to look at."

"Nikki. You can barely keep your eyes opened," he said.

"Ten minutes. I promise," I said.

He nodded and shuffled back upstairs.

I couldn't drop this line of investigation. Neal had talked himself out of the connection and really had no reason to investigate him further. Stan was still looking into Sebastian which left me with Dr. Hubble.

What is the doctor's role?

I reviewed the claims Dr. Hubble had a hand in. Janelle wasn't anywhere in these documents and maybe Will was right, they purposely stayed away from each to not draw attention to their past business.

But everyone else in the therapy center worked with all of the parties involved. They used all the doctors, all the insurance companies and all of the medical supply companies. The lack of cases together raised the hairs on the back of my neck.

I made a list of Janelle's contacts. It was almost three in the morning when I finished the list. Sleep was taking control. But I had to know how Janelle and Dr. Hubble fit together in this scheme. It was here somewhere.

I went through each of Janelle's connections, finding them all online. Of course, when something is missing, it was always the last place one looked. I found myself back at the Adams Medical website. This time, the insurance side of it, where Dr. Hubble sat on the board of appeals. He was the man who approved or denied patient appeals.

That could come in handy if something went wrong or right.

I didn't have access to all of the patient files, and I wasn't finding anything in what Janelle left me to ascertain. How many people may have had their claims denied by the doctor? Would they have blamed Janelle for wrong doing?

My next step was to run queries on Dr. Hubble and while my computer churned out query results for any lawsuits or other improprieties, I climbed in beside Will and was asleep before the queries finished.

***

I woke up, later than I had in years. It was after nine when I came downstairs. Coffee was brewing, Julia was lying on the sofa watching television, Jacob was sorting through my printed query results. They both looked up and pointed to the closed doors to the sunroom.

Cautiously I looked through the glass doors. Emily was crying. Periodically looking at her phone and putting it back in her lap, face down. I knocked on the door.

She glanced up. Her eyes were wet with tears. I opened the door and closed it behind me.

All I could do was sit beside her. She leaned against me, still quietly crying to herself. I don't know how long I sat there with her, but she eventually pulled away.

"Sydney and Lisa," she whispered.

"What about them?"

"They did it. They were the ones telling Marshall where I was."

I kissed her forehead and ran my hand through her hair.

"Why did they do that?"

She pulled away and wiped her cheeks. "They were helping him get back together with me. They thought it was romantic."

My stomach roiled. "They know what he did, right?"

"Yeah. They knew he cheated, and I didn't want to see him again."

"I'm sorry, Em. They sound like they aren't such good friends."

She nodded. "I didn't know it until now. And I'm supposed to room with Lisa in a few weeks. I can't…"

"One step at a time. We'll call the school and see if there are any other rooms. We'll figure it out."

"It's not just that. They were my best friends. And now they're mad at me because I'm mad at them, and they don't think they did anything wrong."

"They disrespected your wishes and crossed your boundaries. They're wrong and you deserve better."

"And I'm the bad one," she grumbled.

"They're feeling guilty and putting it on you to feel better. Eventually you'll find a way to move on. Can I get you anything?"

Emily shook her head. "I just want to stay in here and be mad for a while. After that, I don't know."

"I'm going to get some coffee. I can come back in, and we can talk or we can figure out the rooming thing. Whatever you need," I said.

"I'll be okay. I can call and see about dorm rooms."

"You sure?"

She nodded. "Go do what you need to do."

I kissed her forehead.

"If you need anything, let me know."

"Thanks, Mom."

Her phone buzzed. She glanced at it. "Lisa's trying to apologize." She put her phone down and looked at my expression. "I'm fine."

I knew she wasn't, but Emily had laid back down and curled herself into a ball. She was no longer crying, but she was resolved in her feelings.

"Mom," she said quietly.

"What sweetie?"

"Why are people so sucky?"

I wanted to laugh but held her hand instead. "Because emotions are messy. And people don't often realize they are wrong when they think they're helping. Your friends were misguided in their attempt to help you and Marshall."

"That doesn't help." Emily sat up.

"I know. I'm not sure there's much I can do to make this better. I think this is where time will make it easier."

"That sucks."

Emily leaned against me and we sat that way for many minutes before she pulled away. "Don't you have work to do?"

"I do, but I don't want to leave you like this."

She wiped a stray tear from her cheek. "Go find Janelle's killer. I think I may know what I can do about my living situation." She offered a smile.

I almost believed she was better. "You sure?"

She nodded. "I need to think and do," she held up her phone.

I kissed her cheek and stepped back into the kitchen.

"So, what did you discover?" I said to Jacob.

He glanced up. "Is she okay?"

"I think she will be."

I took a seat beside Jacob as he showed me the computer screen.

"Well, Dr. Hubble has his hands in everything. He's been sued by several patients for falsifying records, denying appeals. He's also been in front of an ethics board more than once." Jacob smiled when he looked up. He was having fun with this.

"How many lawsuits?"

"There's five listed."

He handed me the pile. I skimmed the lawsuits. I knew Jacob had seen it too. Marshall Pointer's parents had sued Dr. Hubble fifteen years ago.

"How does Marshall figure in this?" Jacob asked.

"I think it's a coincidence. But it connects Janelle to Dr. Hubble."

"You sure?" Jacob asked.

"I'm pretty sure, and I haven't found anything to suggest otherwise. Anything else?"

"Sebastian Winston."

My eyes widened. I wanted Sebastian and Jacob so far away from each other they were on different planets. "What about him?"

Jacob pushed a document toward me. "He worked with Dr. Hubble fifteen years ago. But he worked under a different name."

I stared at the form. An old legal filing. The name of Sebatian Cole worked for Dr. Hubble. It could be a coincidence.

"I looked up Sebastian Winston, but there was nothing on him prior to five years ago. I'm jumping to the conclusion he changed his name, and it's the same person," Jacob said.

"What about Sebastian Cole? What did you find on him?" I asked.

"That's the thing. When I looked up Sebastian Cole, he seemed to disappear about ten years ago. Prior to that, he was on the radar. Petty crime. Robbery, check fraud, theft. Small time stuff, a few stints in jail."

"If it's the same person he was off the radar for about five years," I noted.

I reviewed what Jacob had found on Sebastian Cole including a mug shot. I pulled out the pictures I had of Sebastian and Katrina from St. Thomas and stared at the two pictures. If you didn't look carefully enough, you could mistake them for two different men.

"Same nose, eye color, similar build. What did Sebastian Cole get himself into?" I handed Jacob the pictures.

"I did good?" he asked.

"With English, no. With this yes. Though you really shouldn't be helping me. The only reason I didn't stop it is because you helped when I got the USB drive. I don't want you involved. There are some bad people involved in this."

"There always are," he quipped.

"Thanks for the added investigating."

"I want to help you find Janelle's killer. I knew her too. And I like it. It's a great big puzzle that needs to be worked out. And I think I understand what's going on."

"You worked out something?"

He nodded and smiled. "It's like Sebastian was this petty criminal and got caught several times. Maybe one time he got caught in a really big way. He's working for Dr. Hubble legitimately or the doc sought him out because of the trouble. And that meeting changed Sebastian's life. He started working for the doc after changing his name, becomes a new person in a new life," Jacob said.

"It's a good theory," I said.

"It is."

"If Sebastian was loyal to the doctor maybe he rose in the ranks of the fraud scheme. He brings the doctor in. But it doesn't prove they killed Janelle or Marvin Gartner. It's the strongest theory I have though. And because of that, please stop looking into it. I really don't want you in this at all."

"Only the behind-the-scenes stuff. I promise," he said.

"I'm serious Jacob. No more digging. I really appreciate you reviewing the queries, but please don't do anything else. I'm serious."

"You're really scared," he said surprised.

"Yeah. Sebastian appears to be dangerous."

"I promise. But if I see something in your research, I'll let you know."

I wasn't sure how much to admonish him, but he had been helpful. Having said that, I was still scared. I wanted to get that through his head. I was hoping he understood.

Jacob must have seen it in my expression. "I promise, Mom. I'll be careful. Not researching outside of the house. Just what you give me. I promise. You really think it's that bad?"

“Janelle is dead. I think it’s serious. Everyone involved can find out I’ve had a hand in this. The DEA knows. Sebastian is high up and involved in big things. He probably changed his name because something big was coming his way.”

“And this is that big?”

I nodded.

He put the papers in one of the folders. “I’ll be careful.”

“Go hang out with friends. Have fun.”

Julia, tired of her television show, walked into the kitchen. “Why does he get to help?”

“He doesn’t get to help. Jacob was in the right place at the right time. But now he’s gonna go hang out. You should too.”

“Ugh. So unfair.”

“Uh huh. It’s summertime. Go have fun.”

“Movie downstairs?” Jacob asked.

“I’m game,” Emily said from behind us. Her eyes were still wet and red, but she was up and moving. I considered that progress.

“Fine.”

It had been a weird ending to my late morning as the kids headed downstairs. Whatever it was they’d be doing, I was glad they were doing it together.

CHAPTER 17

I spent the day cleaning up the house and completing background checks just in time for another late night with Stan.

It was after nine that night, when I left the kids and Will at home, watching a movie I wish I could have seen with them. But tonight, I met Stan at the office.

I walked in. It wasn't what I had expected, though I wasn't sure what I was expecting.

The walls were beige, the carpet once was beige, now greyish with years of foot traffic. One old metal desk sat across from the door where a receptionist once sat. Now the desk was empty, clean, and without the normal office equipment, except the desk lamp, blotter, and pencil cup holder.

Stan's office door was open and from the front door I could see his desk, cluttered with papers and folders, an old Styrofoam container. I walked inside. "Hi, Stan," I said. He looked up from his folder and smiled, held out his hand, offering me a chair.

"Randy will be here soon. He said he had something and wanted to talk in private."

I raised my eyebrows. What could possibly need to be discussed in person and not over the phone?

"Did he give you any indication he cracked it?"

Stan laughed. "He cracked it. Most people aren't that bright, and I'm guessing we could have figured it out on our own."

The door opened; footsteps crossed the floor. A guy of average height and weight walked in, wearing khakis and a collared shirt. Not what I imagined, but then what I imagined was probably a stereotype. I've been learning to ignore those.

"Randy, this is Nikki Page. Nikki? Randy," Stan said.

I shook his hand; he took a seat beside me with just a nod.

"So, yeah, Stan. Next time send me something hard," Randy smiled.

I chuckled. It was just as Stan suggested it might be. And for all of that, Stan shrugged.

"Okay. Give it to us."

Randy pulled a small notebook from his back pocket and tossed it to Stan. Stan read, glanced at me.

"Now here's the thing, Nikki. Sometimes we need to bring in the police. This is a meeting notice for two days from now. 1:30 am. Does this look familiar to you?" He tossed me the notebook.

"Drug drop?" I asked, but neither man seemed to have an answer to that.

"Why?" Stan asked.

"Because of Lester Roland and the DEA watching my house."

"That's heavy, and I'm outta here," Randy said.

"Thank you," I said as he offered a mock salute and turned, leaving Stan and I alone in the office.

"Well, that bothered him," I said.

"It should. And I'm sure it scares you too."

I nodded. "Knowing the DEA was looking at Sebastian scared me. He's expanding the business, using the medical fraud to either buy the drugs or use it to procure them to sell on the black market."

"Have you researched that at all?" Stan asked.

"Everyone has been telling me to stay clear of Sebastian. I've done that. Now I'll let Lester Roland know about this."

I took a picture of the notebook and attached that and the picture of the original note to Mr. Roland at the DEA and hit send.

I was hoping that would be enough for whatever the DEA needed to do.

"So why did Sebastian have Janelle and Marvin Gartner killed?" Stan asked.

I shrugged. "If they were doing so well with the plan, I can only figure they killed Janelle because she was working with the FBI and Marvin, maybe he was too. I suppose we could always check out his apartment and see what he knew."

I glanced at Stan; he raised his eyebrows. "I'll come with you on that one. Let's try and get in tomorrow. What else did you find out?"

I gave him a copy of all my notes about the connection between Dr. Hubble, Janelle, Marshall Pointer, Neal Enders, and Sebastian Cole.

"And your concern is Dr. Hubble, Sebastian, and Janelle knew each other all those years ago?"

"Janelle and the doctor are connected through Adams Medical. Sebastian is connected to him from that early time together."

"Does it change any theories?" Stan asked.

"Instead of Sebastian bringing in Janelle through the speech therapy contact, maybe it was Dr. Hubble who brought them together."

"Sebastian was there because the doctor told him to be there?"

I nodded.

"It's one more piece, as you said. One more connection."

My phone buzzed. It was a text message from Agent Lester. How?

Long story, but that's what we found, I replied.

Do not attend!

I'm not planning on being there.

"The DEA?"

"They're taking it seriously. I'm not sure if I feel better, though." I sighed. I was tired. I was scared. I sent one more text to Will. The house was still being watched.

I breathed a sigh of relief, but it was only a small one.

"Tomorrow, Marvin Gartner's apartment?"

"I'll pick you up around eleven, and we'll head over there. If anything else comes up, let me know."

He shut down his computer and the lights and walked me to the car. He watched me as I pulled out of the parking lot and drove away.

***

Two late nights in a row for me, and I was dragging. The house was quiet when I returned home, the kids were asleep in their rooms, and Will was watching tv in the den.

He turned to me. "We have a new team outside. Something about a stake out or change of plans. They weren't very specific."

I sat on the edge of the couch. "Our code breaker came up with something useful. That's good. Maybe this will end soon," I said.

"You're close. You always get there in the end." He reached for my hands and pulled me into his lap.

"It's nice you all have so much faith in me. I'm worried this is our life. Always in danger. I can't put the kids in that position. Or you." I lay my head on his shoulder.

"It does seem to happen quite a bit to you, doesn't it?"

He was smiling when I looked up at him. "That's not funny."

"No. Sorry. I know it's not. We're in this because you hit a nerve. That's good. And the DEA and the police know about it. Hopefully whatever they're doing in the next few days bears useful clues."

"I hope so too." I yawned and pushed away. "I'm going to bed. You coming up?"

"In a bit. I was enjoying the quiet."

I kissed his cheek and dragged myself up to bed. Tomorrow was gonna be another interesting day. I just didn't know it yet.

***

Stan pulled up in a blue four door sedan, and I climbed in beside him.

"Presumably, the police have been through there, so we should have no trouble," he said as he pulled away.

It was a quick ride to Marvin Gartner's house. A condo really. Stan walked in as if he belonged in the building and sidled up to the receptionist.

"Good morning, ma'am. I'm Stan Marley," he said and offered half a fake salute.

"Yes. How can I help you?"

He handed her his ID.

"You're a PI?" she asked. Her face was youngish, though her hair was nearly gray. She was wide eyed at the sight of a PI.

"I am. I'm working a case. This is my associate, Nikki Page."

"Hi." I said as I joined him at the desk.

"How can I help you?" she said.

"We're investigating Marvin Gartner's death, and I'm hoping you'll let us upstairs." He pointed his chin toward the elevators.

"Marvin. Poor Marvin. We're so shocked. He was such a nice man. He always left at 7:25 and came back home at 5:45. On the dot. Clock work. Always so nice."

"Did he ever have anyone come see him here? Someone who stood out, perhaps?" Stan asked.

She stuck out her tongue and looked past us as she thought about it. "Not when I was on duty. I can't say for sure when I wasn't here. Do you have any idea of who might have killed him?" she asked, genuine concern in his voice.

"We have suspects, but nothing definite," I said. "Did he have a girlfriend, boyfriend that he ever spoke about, someone who looked like they belonged here?"

She smiled. "He did talk about a girl. Woman, I guess. Someone he liked very much. But she never came here. No one did. Not while I was on duty."

"Does she have a name?" I asked.

"I don't remember. He so kindly spoke of a very dear woman who was helping him with a problem, and he'd blush. Wait… maybe it was a Lynnette. Or Jeanette. I'm sorry I can't remember."

I looked at Stan. He raised his eyebrows.

"Could her name have been Janelle?" Stan asked.

The receptionist's eyes widened. "That's it. It was Janelle. I got the impression they weren't dating. He might have been smitten though."

"Did anyone ever call here for Marvin, asking for him, or asking if he was home?" Stan asked.

"Nope."

"Any packages ever arrive for him? Either large or envelope sized?" Stan asked.

"Usually larger envelope packages. I've signed for several of those over the years," she said proudly.

"Do you remember who they were from?" I asked.

This time she tapped her finger to her chin. "Let's see. I don't remember off hand who they were from. I just remember they were from medical supply companies, doctors mostly. I thought he might be sick. A chronic thing but he always seemed so healthy… oh, wait."

She turned around. Behind her was a credenza and a large top drawer. She opened it up and pulled out a ledger. "Duh. We keep track of this in case our residents need something. And to protect ourselves if we sign for them."

She opened the ledger and looked through the entries. "Here. Here." She turned the ledger toward us and pointed to several entries. It appeared Marvin was receiving regular envelopes from several medical companies and doctors, including Adams Medical where he worked.

I whipped out my phone and took several pictures of entries dating back a year. "Thanks for this. It will help figure out who killed him," I said.

She smiled widely and put the book back.

"Can we go upstairs, now?" Stan asked.

***

The receptionist we now know as Cyndy with two 'y's, let us go upstairs without written permission from a resident. We found Marvin's condo on the sixth floor and stood in front of the locked door, with crime scene tape still across it.

Stan was on his knees, jimmying the lock with his lock pick kit.

"When do I learn how to do that?"

He glanced up at me and grimaced before returning to his work.

"When you get your hours, we'll celebrate with a lesson," he said and the lock popped open.

When he stood, his knees creaked, and he led me inside the condo.

It was unremarkable. Beige sofa, carpet, drapes, and walls. There was a framed poster over the sofa of a forest view, no pictures of friends or family or trinkets from vacations. It was perfectly acceptable for a rental property, but not a home. I followed Stan's lead as we walked around the front room opening drawers, searching the contents. What I noticed was a neatly staged house with organized items in the drawers and on the one set of bookshelves.

We walked into the kitchen and did the same thing with the drawers and cabinets. I was pretty sure that anything worth anything was already found by the police when they searched after his death. We continued anyway.

We entered the only bedroom. One bed, one bedside table, a lamp, a small closet and bathroom. There was nothing in the dresser drawers except for clothes. Any of his documents from the medical supply companies were already at the police unless…

"If Marvin spoke of Janelle because they had some relationship, I wonder if she told him her secret hiding spots." I opened the closet again and knelt down. I pulled on the carpet, until I found the loose corner and pulled it away.

"Good work. But how did you know?" Stan asked, slightly impressed.

"Will told me Janelle did this, and that's how I found her stash."

Stan sat beside me as I pulled documents out of a space between two joists. There was no safe, but there was all of his evidence. Claim forms, letters from Sebastian on what to do when a certain client came into Murphy's. It was all there.

I found a bag on Marvin's shelf, and we placed all of what he had in his hiding spot, into the bag. As I did, I skimmed each page. Much of what I found was the same as what Janelle had. I even saw correspondence between Janelle and Marvin about going to the FBI.

"It didn't sound like Marvin was working with the FBI. But Janelle was trying to get him to come forward too."

"They must have both liked each other," Stan said as he took the letter from me and put it into the bag. "Check and see if there's any other locations under that carpet and then we'll go."

I did as he asked and found nothing more. We exited the apartment, locked it up and headed out. When we got downstairs, Cyndy with two 'y's was chatting up a young man, and we slipped out without her noticing.

CHAPTER 18

Going through Marvin Gartner's files wasn't an exciting job. Much of what he had I had already seen through Janelle's paperwork. It was as if he was keeping duplicates for safe keeping. While they could have worked on the same client files, my guess was Janelle asked him to keep copies just in case.

If Marvin really liked her, I'm sure he had no problem holding on to the documents. Unfortunately, I didn't find anything new amongst what he had.

I took a sip of tea as I turned over a new document and skimmed another claim form. My phone rang, and I glanced at the screen. Neal Enders.

Huh?

"This is Nikki," I said trying to mask my confusion.

"Hi, Nikki. Neal Enders here," he said and added a nervous laugh. "I hope I'm not interrupting important work."

"No. Not at all. How can I help you?"

"I feel awful and after that weird coincidence, I keep thinking about my time with Janelle. I know it ended, but I cared about her, both times we dated. I've been thinking about her murder. It's all I can think about. Trying to remember calls, mysterious visitors." He was quiet, contemplative as he gave me his rationale for calling.

I didn't expect I'd get anything new.

"And you remembered something?" I was trying to keep the skepticism out of my voice.

"I did. It was almost insignificant. I suppose that's why I forgot about it. One night, she answered her phone but hung up right away. She left the room and returned shortly thereafter. It happened two more times that evening. I thought maybe a prank caller because she was bothered by it."

"Do you know why she left the room? Did she indicate at all that something was going on?"

"Well. That's the thing. She went to the bathroom, and I went to the kitchen. I saw the notebook she kept in there. The date was listed, next to a name. I wish I could remember, but I thought it had to do with a client."

"You don't remember the dates, do you?" I asked.

"I wish I could remember. It's been years since that happened. I just thought you should know there was odd behavior when we were together."

"Anything else? Other odd behavior or people?"

"Yes. I've been remembering strange things that I didn't think about until she died. She would look out the window at times as if she were looking for someone. Sometimes she'd be upset and sometimes relieved. That was more recent. Do you think any of these matters?"

"It confirms something was going on with her. If anything," I said. But we already knew that.

Without knowing the exact dates, I couldn't compare it to the phone records to make those connections.

"I was wondering if we could speak in person," Neal said.

"What? I… do you have something you need to show me?"

"It's just, after speaking with you I remember things. More things I just assumed were innocuous events. I think it would help. You could tell me where you are in all of this mess."

I wondered why he was suddenly interested in helping me find her killer. When I first reached out, he gave me what he could, and I found it helpful as background information. Was he worried about something or did his connection to Janelle really get him to start thinking about it, seriously thinking about what he may have noticed.

For now, I'd give him the benefit of the doubt.

"I'm not able to meet right now. Maybe next week. But you can call me anytime you remember something. I'm still investigating."

"And you have no idea who killed her?"

"The police are looking at several people and have an idea who may have killed her. But there's just not enough evidence and the police are still waiting for the results of some of the tests."

It was mostly the truth. For now, the police were looking at Sebastian for her murder and I was blindsided by the evidence he was most likely the murderer.

But as I went through Marvin Gartner's documents, I found nothing new. I was stuck on Sebastian with a small possibility George Egan killed Janelle and Marvin. But the police still couldn't find George, so everything was up in the air. Except now we knew Marvin died before Janelle. What did that tell us? I sighed.

"Did you ever meet Marvin Gartner?" I asked on a whim.

"Marvin? Yeah. I met him. Once or twice. Janelle dropped some papers off to him. I met him on one of those times."

"What did you think of him?"

"I really didn't. Though I think he liked Janelle. Really liked her. Though, I don't think they had anything romantic.

He wasn't her type. But he really liked her. Was willing to help her. You don't think he killed her because she wouldn't date him, do you?"

I stifled a laugh. I shouldn't have laughed at all.

"No. He was murdered before Janelle."

"Oh," he said quietly. "I'm sorry to hear that. He seemed like a nice man."

A nice man. Why was he killed then? It didn't appear that he was in charge of anything. It was Janelle who was directing the investigation with the FBI and Marvin was merely doing his part. Why kill him too?

"Thanks for calling and helping fill in some pieces. If you remember any of the dates these calls happened, please let me know. I'm trying to find out who called her and when. It would help narrow it down."

"Yes. I can do that. Let me look through my calendar. See if I can get you those dates. Thanks for talking to me."

"No problem, Mr. Enders. Thanks again for your help."

I was familiar with the idea of writing up my phone calls with clients for the record. While I had taken time to make notes on all my witness interviews, I was careful with this one because of his connection to Janelle, both past and present and now his interest in the case.

It didn't take long for Neal to send me two dates and times.

I found the phone records. Both calls belonged to the burner phone. No surprise there seeing that most of the calls we assumed were Sebastian but not on his phone.

I thanked Neal for his help, but all this did was confirm she received these weird, less than a minute phone calls. I searched the rest of the bills for any other short calls. There were several through the months. Too many for me to assume they were wrong numbers or spam. Was this a clue to how she got her instructions? Did the caller give her a name, an instruction, a code word?

It was indeed strange, but it was something. I sent an email about this to Detective Clyde and another to Lester Roland. Maybe they could get phone records to confirm this was an ongoing process. I'm not sure it would help or get us closer to Janelle's killer.

***

"I think you're right," Stan Marley said to me when I told him what I planned to do with George Egan's wife.

"Do you want to come with me?" I asked. I was looking through some paperwork Detective Clyde had on the whereabouts of George Egan. He was still missing and yet the police were looking at him for the murders of Janelle and Marvin.

"Yes. I do. You're still in your apprenticeship, and the fact we haven't looked at him yet seems like a good time to do it, yeah?"

"I agree. I think we assumed he ran because Janelle and Marvin were murdered. He went missing after Janelle was discovered."

"If he killed Marvin then Janelle, he skipped town and hid."

"If he didn't kill them, he's in hiding because he thinks he's next. Based on the police notes, he's not using his credit cards or accessing his bank. They can't find him moving large sums of money prior to any of this, but his wife said there's a lot of money missing in one of their accounts. So that's how he's living, but where is he living?"

"He's probably dead," Stan said.

"Probably. The police haven't come close to finding him."

"Then you should look," he said.

I had found Sabrina and Melanie Crew where he couldn't. I got lucky and found the clue that led me to them. Would Mrs. Egan have that one clue when we finally spoke to her?

"I'll set up something for tomorrow, and we can head over there."

"Good thinking, Nikki. I'll pick you up when you get me a time," he said and hung up.

I called Madeline Egan.

After explaining who I was, she asked, "You're trying to find George?" she asked softly.

"Yes. I'm trying to find him and figure out who killed Janelle and Marvin," I added.

"Marvin? Who's he?" she asked, genuinely confused.

"Marvin Gartner was killed before Janelle was killed, and we think he was killed by the same person."

"Oh. Do you think that person did something to George?" she asked. Her voice was small, soft, and almost childlike. I didn't know her, but I thought it could be the stress.

"We don't know. But that is a possibility. I was hoping I could see you tomorrow and ask a few questions. Would that be possible?"

"Why not just ask on the phone? It seems like such trouble."

My brain was wired and knew I should push an in-person meeting, but I had her on the phone now.

"What do you think happened to your husband? To George?"

"I think whatever he and Janelle got themselves into scared him. Her death terrified him, and he ran to protect himself."

"Did he take money? Clothes? How's he living?" I asked.

"Oh. We had cash in the safe here. He took what we had. It was quite a lot. About $100,000. He's going to set us up somewhere away from those bad people who killed Janelle."

"Did George tell you what he was into? What happened?"

"No. No he didn't want me to get involved. He only told me that Janelle had brought bad people into the center, and he was forced to work for them to keep his job. Don't get me wrong. He loved Janelle like a daughter and was very protective of her. He was trying to protect her and us when he joined whatever it was. And now he's gone," she said quietly.

"Do you know where he went?"

"I'm not sure. He told me he was leaving. Packed up the car and left."

"Do you have any vacation or rental property he might be staying at?"

"Umm. We did. But I thought we sold off all of the property holdings. He could have kept one."

Why wouldn't she know? That's marital property. Or was she being evasive? Did George have secrets?

"Did the police ask you the same questions?"

"Yes. I told them the same. They emptied the cabinets. Took what they thought would help find George. They haven't, yet, you know."

"I know. I can call them and see where the investigation is on finding George."

"That would be helpful. I'm waiting for word. He left with all that money, and I worry something happened."

I can only imagine. That's a lot of cash.

"Thank you for your time, Mrs. Egan. If you think of anything, can you call me at this number?"

"I will. Thank you for thinking of George. With all that happened to Janelle, I fear he's not being looked for."

"It's my job to look at all the pieces. I'm happy to look for him. Thank you for your time."

I texted Stan when I got off the phone with her.

I could imagine him rolling his eyes as he thanked me for trying to get something out of her.

I had this feeling that George, if he was alive, wasn't far away. I also had a sense that he was closely tied to someone in the plan.

I searched for property records for George Egan, George Madeline, Madeline Egan, George and Madeline Egan but if he owned any property aside from his main residence, nothing was pinging.

While I was at it, I checked the same thing with Janelle and Marvin. Again, nothing came up.

My trusty databases might not have provided anything, and for the hell of it, I tried the internet and searched for George Egan.

There were no articles about car accidents with a man his age or arrests with the suspect matching his description. I'm sure the police had gone down that alley. Without speaking with Madeline Egan and seeing the house and getting a feel for her and them as a couple, I couldn't glean anything else.

George would be hard to find, without leaving a paper trail. What if Madeline lied and was in contact with him, but she didn't know where he was. Or did she know?

I left my computer at home and hopped in the car and headed to George and Madeline Egan's house. If I had to, I'd come up with new questions I wanted to ask her just to take a peek.

Traffic was light in the middle of the afternoon, and I wasn't sure what I was going to accomplish by sitting outside of the Egan's house. My gut told me Madeline knew more than she was saying or there was something in the house.

I stared at George Egan's home. He and his wife had done well for themselves. The house was a mansion. Three stories, white stucco and looked as though it could have fit into the French countryside.

The yard was impeccably manicured, the paint pristine, and the summer flowers were colorfully in bloom.

The rest of the neighborhood was the same.

I watched youngish moms or nannies pushing strollers, a jogger, and a delivery van pull into the neighbor's house. It looked like any other suburb outside of Chicago. I knew this was my future life once I pursued the private investigator route, so I waited through the boredom, realized I should have brought a snack or water. At least I wouldn't need a bathroom anytime soon.

A Mercedes sedan pulled into the Egan's house, the garage door slowly opened and patiently Madeline waited to be able to drive inside. She closed the garage door.

Is that it?

I glanced around the neighborhood where people headed up and down the street. One looked at me, questioning why I was there, but she quickly walked away from my car.

I sat back, pulled out my phone and turned on the camera. I waited.

Why was I here?

I reminded myself I'd be heading inside to speak with Madeline again, but in the meantime, I wanted to see the traffic that came and went down the street or to the house.

Madeline came back out and walked the short distance from the house to the mailbox. I sat up and snapped some pictures with my phone. Not sure why, but I continued to shoot as she shuffled through the pile of mail she received, stopping on a particular envelope. Her eyes widened; her hands trembled. She looked around as if thinking someone was watching her. Besides me.

I kept shooting pictures.

Even when she didn't see who she thought might be there,

she hightailed it back to the house, slamming the door behind her, I took pictures.

Did I learn anything?

Possibly. If the letter was from George, a blackmailer, or a threat of some kind, she might be scared. What was in that letter?

I stepped out of the car, glanced around the neighborhood trying to figure out what Madeline had been looking for. I walked across the street and looked between the houses. No one was there, that shouldn't have been.

I walked up the driveway to the front door and knocked. I could hear footsteps leading to the door, and then nothing. I waited; it didn't seem as though Madeline was going to chance it and open the door. I took that to mean she was frightened and not knowing me would add to that. I knocked again.

"Madeline. It's Nikki Page. I'd like to ask you some more questions," I shouted.

Locks clicked and the door squeaked opened.

Madeline was crying. "He's dead," she said as she held out the envelope she had just received.

CHAPTER 19

I shuffled through the photos Madeline received. It was clearly a dead body lying on the floor, with a bullet hole through the chest. Just like Janelle. I hadn't seen the photos of Marvin's crime scene, but my guess is, he was killed the same way. I could be wrong though.

My hands trembled as I scrutinized each of them. There were ten photos in total, but not all were of the dead body. Some were pictures of George Egan, his battered body tied to a chair, a hood over his head. Others were of George tied to a chair, blindfolded with his hands tied behind his back.

What I noticed immediately was if Madeline hadn't told me these pictures were of George, I wouldn't have known. While I did see pictures of him alive, I couldn't confirm this was him.

But if she says so…

"And you're absolutely sure it's him?"

"It… those are his pants, his tie. He's… he's tied up…" She shuddered and began to wail.

I dropped the photos on the table and went to her, placing my arms around her frail frame. "I'm so sorry for your loss."

I caught a look at the pictures scattered on the table. No matter the angle, I couldn't tell if it was actually him. Was the body shape how she knew it was him or just the clothes? Anyone could have taken his clothes and put them on a dead body. Did he kill that body and use it to fake his own death?

"Would you like me to call the police for you?"

She moved away from me. "Yes. Yes. I think that would be a good idea. Thank you, Nikki. I know you came here for more information and now this…" She nearly fell into the chair as she slumped against the back of it.

I called the police.

I was anxious as I waited. I texted Stan.

Why did you go there?

I could almost hear the anger in his question.

I looked out the window. My attention returned to the pictures still on the table.

"Madeline. I know this is distressing, but is there anything in the pictures you recognize? The carpet, the walls? Do you recognize anything?" I asked her.

I felt bad for interrogating her under the circumstances, but I had to know. I had to find out how the pieces fit together.

I wasn't sure if it this would help find Janelle's killer, but I didn't know which clues would crack this case.

"I… I don't know."

Madeline surprised me and picked up the pictures, taking her time with each one. She was trembling but didn't stop searching for clues.

"I… I think this is the cabin we used to go to. Weekends and such. I have the address here."

She stumbled to the desk in the living room, a traditional space, filled with formal antiques, highly sophisticated paintings, statues, and other vintage collectables. Their house was lovely. Stuffy but lovely.

She neatly wrote out the address and handed it to me.

"The police will want to know as well."

She offered a nervous smile, sighed deeply and sat herself on the sofa.

"Can I get you a glass of water?"

She glanced around the room. "Maybe some bourbon. Over there." She pointed to the sideboard, glasses neatly stacked, the bottles lined up against the wall.

I poured her one and handed it to her with just enough time for the police to arrive.

I let them in. Not only were the local police there, so was Benson Clyde. He nodded and walked inside. I led them to Madeline who slowly sipped her drink.

I kept to the side of the room waiting for the police to look through the pictures. She told them what she told me, gave them the address to the cabin in Wisconsin. Detective Clyde joined me.

"What do you think?" he asked.

"I've seen pictures of him when he was alive. I wouldn't think those pictures were him. But then I wasn't married to him," I said. I watched as the police continued to look through papers and files in their new search.

"I agree with you. I think he ran after he killed Janelle or Marvin, and this is his way of sneaking away for good. We'll know for sure when we get to the body."

I glanced at him. "What do you mean, Janelle or Marvin?"

He pulled out a folder from the bag slung across his shoulder and handed it to me.

I opened the cover and scanned the police report. "They believe Janelle and Marvin were killed by different people?"

"Two different guns were used and there are different biologicals found on each body. DNA was run on the samples, and they are different people. Two men by the way."

"That could mean there are two assassins in the organization. Maybe more. Keep each killing separate. Confound the police," I said.

"Either way, we have two killers on the loose. Possibly a third in the murder of our missing witness," he said, tersely. "I don't have to warn you again to be careful." He turned and walked in the group of police officers to get their impressions and help with the search.

I continued to watch as they wound down their search. A detective broke free of the group and headed my way.

"Mrs. Page. I'm Detective Davis. Detective Clyde vouched for you. Can I ask you why you're here?"

"I'm investigating Janelle's murder, and it occurred to me that maybe Mrs. Egan had information on where her husband was. I was starting to think he had some involvement in Janelle's murder rather than being another victim. It appears I might have been wrong about that," I said.

"A DNA test has been ordered," Detective Davis said. "Do you have any other theories?"

I explained what I had said to Detective Clyde. Detective Davis just nodded. "You think he was involved in one of the other murders and ran? If he did fake his death that would be a great way to escape jail." He grimaced.

"But the DNA tests will prove whether or not it's him," I reminded him, though I didn't really need to. "Or there is more than one assassin in this group. At least I can see Sebastian needing them with what he does," I suggested.

"What do you think happened to Janelle?" he asked me.

"I think she was too far inside the organization and wanted out. She went to the FBI with the evidence, and she was killed for it. Marvin was killed for it; my guess is because he was fond of Janelle, and I think he was helping her. And George, that remains to be seen."

"I was asked to keep you informed on the murder of George Egan; however, it turns out."

"Thanks. I'm curious to find out what's really going on."

Detective Davis walked away. I hadn't learned much, but now they think there are two killers. How deep did this crime ring go?

***

It seemed so simple when I started looking into Janelle's murder. She was in too deep and wanted out, and she was killed for it.

Now we had three deaths, at least two killers and the DEA searching for someone in the organization who not only worked in insurance fraud but also drugs. While it wasn't cocaine, heroin or morphine, the drugs in question were fentanyl, oxycontin, and even pain relievers with codeine, all ill gotten through the insurance fraud.

I typed up what I had learned and what I thought and sent it off to Stan. I clocked my hours and sat back. He sent a quick text.

Nice work.

It didn't feel like nice work. It felt awful. I knew other cases wouldn't be like this; I wouldn't know the murder victim.

But I did feel awful. I closed my eyes and took a deep breath. It was time to put it aside and work on something else. But the ringing phone broke my concentration. It was Neal Enders.

Again?

"Hi Neal," I said. My voice was tired, my heart anguished.

"Oh no. Did you learn something?" he said without saying hello.

"I don't have any idea who killed her. We're learning about new connections but haven't pinpointed her murderer."

"Oh," he said quietly. "I'm just so hopeful you'll find her killer and her family can find peace."

He was taking an interest in the case, more so now than he had when I first interviewed him. I wondered what the reason was for that.

"I don't mean to seem harsh, but you didn't take that much interest in the case until I called you about knowing Janelle fifteen years ago. Can I ask why?"

He was quiet. A little too quiet. He finally said, "After you found out about me knowing Janelle, I couldn't stop thinking about all of it. Her and I back then and getting back together. I really loved her and when she was killed, it just intensified. And now, I just want it over for her. For her parents."

I could hear the stress and tears in his voice. While I believed him, there was something in my gut that told me this was getting way out of hand, and I was missing something. I was hoping something would come to me when the DNA results came in.

"I'm sorry for your loss. I wish I had something to tell you. I just don't right now," I said.

"I'm sorry I'm bothering you. I just feel so helpless," Neal said.

"I know the feeling. But you can call anytime. Hopefully next time, I'll have some news."

After saying goodbye, I followed my gut and pulled out my computer and searched for Neal Enders.

***

He was clean. No convictions, only drunk and disorderly all the way back in college, thirty years ago. He had no lawsuits against him or against anyone else, he never had a traffic ticket. That, I found odd. What adult never got caught?

I continued to dig.

He had a nice house, according to his profiles on social media, he had a good paying job he had been at for fifteen years.

Neal Enders life seemed straight as an arrow. He worked, he played, he traveled, he loved.

As I deep dove into his social media, specifically the pictures, I noticed that there had been more than the first time I looked. More Janelle. Was he in love with her or was he obsessed with her?

I had my answer when I read his most recent posts.

My dearest Janelle. I can't eat or sleep as I think of her. I miss her so much. Her life was taken; it was too short.

There were more posts like that. More professing his deep love for her. They had dated in college for a year, she cheated on him, and they broke up. They were friends again fifteen years ago, and most recently they dated for three months. But again, she had treated him poorly and had broken up again.

Had he been a placeholder until someone better came around? Did he do things for her because he was in love with her and would do anything for her? Much like Marvin? Marvin died because of it, but was Janelle killed because of it?

Maybe we had it wrong. Maybe Marvin was killed because of the insurance fraud. He was killed first and maybe he was killed to scare Janelle into staying in the scheme. And maybe she was killed because she hurt someone badly and that someone wanted to make the police believe she was killed for the same reason. He used Marvin's death to hide the true murderer.

Could it be that simple?

Could Neal Enders have killed Janelle because he loved her, and she didn't love him? Was Neal Enders the killer all along?

CHAPTER 20

With Stan sitting in the driver's seat with me beside him, he watched Neal Enders' house, and I re-read the notes I had taken.

They weren't all that exciting.

"He met Janelle in college. They dated. He claims they were in love, but she cheated on him, and they eventually broke up."

"That's a habit," Stan said. He tensed as a car drove closer to Neal's house.

The car moved on.

My phone buzzed. I glanced at the text; it was yet another from the kids. It had been like this all day. Their squabbles were getting intense again. I texted Jacob back and told him to leave Emily alone.

"Who's texting?" Stan asked as another car drove down the street and drove past us.

"Just my kids. Anyway, Janelle and Neal reconnected years later. Fifteen years ago. I don't think they were dating but they were hanging out. And again, after Janelle asked for a divorce, they started dating. It was great until it wasn't anymore. Neal told me she compared him to Will."

Again, my phone buzzed. It was Emily. I sighed heavily and texted her that I was working, and they needed to figure it out on their own.

I returned to my notes. "Sorry. They've been fighting for the last few weeks. So, I was… okay. Neal told me Janelle's behavior was odd. He said she became mean. Told him he didn't dress well enough; he didn't make as much money as her ex-husband, and he wasn't as good as him."

I shuffled through some screen shots. "I pulled up his social media. It's all over it. He loved her or was obsessed with her. I suppose her treatment and not loving him like he loved her could have been enough to kill her."

"People kill for less," Stan said.

My phone buzzed again. I read the message and texted back to all three kids at once.

I'm working. Go to your own rooms, leave each other alone, and I'll be home when I get home!!!!

I sat back and looked out the window, staring at Neal Enders house. "Sorry about my kids and the texting."

"You're a mom. I get it. You'll figure out how to work cases and handle your kids with practice. Did you ever hear back from Clyde about the letters and which computers and printers they were created on?"

I had talked to Detective Clyde earlier in the day and asked for the results, and to tell him about my theory on Neal Enders. I hadn't heard until my phone rang, at that moment.

"Well, that's creepy. It's Clyde. This is Nikki," I said as I put the call on speaker.

"Mrs. Page. Thank you for that tip. It explains why the letters were neither written on Will Mann's or Janelle Mann's computers and neither were they printed on their printers. We were stumped until your theory," he said. He was neither flippant, nor apologetic, just honest.

"I'm glad it puts some perspective on your case."

"Have you confronted Mr. Enders about this yet?"

"I questioned his interest in the case, but he talked himself out of being a suspect. I'm still not convinced."

"It's looking like a crime of opportunity. If he was mad enough, he could very well used Marvin's murder to disguise Janelle's. We assumed it was the same murderer, based on what Marvin and Janelle had done, but now that we know there were two killers. This fills in the who."

"Any results on biologicals found on Janelle?"

"We're still waiting. In the meantime, I'm waiting on the search warrant. Be careful and don't do anything stupid," Clyde said.

"I'll be careful." I glanced at Stan. He shrugged as he watched Neal's house and the car that pulled into his driveway. "Gotta go. I'm working on something for my boss."

Detective Clyde hung up before I could say goodbye. I pulled out a picture of Neal Enders. The man parked his car outside of his closed garage and stepped out to check his mailbox. I compared him to the picture.

"It's definitely Neal," I said as we watched him enter his house through the front door.

Odd…

Stan watched the second-floor windows.

I pulled out my own binoculars and trained them on the second-floor windows as well. I noticed why Stan had done that when I Neal walked across the window and back again. He was brushing his hair.

Nice binoculars, I thought.

"What do you notice?" Stan asked me. I concentrated on Neal as he walked across the window and back again.

"He's walking around what's probably his bedroom. He was brushing his hair so he might be getting ready to go out. He also parked outside his closed garage and entered through his front door. I only do that when I'm coming back out shortly. Either you were really lucky picking tonight, or you did something to figure out that he was going out."

"Not my first rodeo, and I didn't want to guess since we're working with the police on this. I called his secretary asking for a meeting at 5 pm. I was told he had dinner plans and asked if we could schedule for tomorrow."

"That's brilliant. I'll make sure I remember that trick," I said as I stifled a laugh.

Neal had been in his house for thirty minutes. When he went in, he was wearing khaki pants and a denim collared shirt. When he came out, he was wearing jeans, a t-shirt, a blazer, and loafers. His hair was brushed, and he had shaved. Great binoculars.

He drove away in his Jeep.

"Ready?" Stan asked.

"As I'll ever be."

***

Night was falling, dropping the residential street in shadows, making it more difficult to get our details straight should the police ask who came to the house.

A trick to not drawing suspicion to us was to act as though we belonged there, and when we exited the car, we walked directly to Neal's house, up the stairs to the front door, and pushed the doorbell. I knocked on the front door and looked inside the window beside it. While we knew he wasn't home, we wanted to verify there were no dogs, or other people in the house. We were fairly certain we were alone.

Stan checked the storm door, under the mat, and in the dirt for hollow rocks, while I continued to look inside the windows as if we were still waiting for the owner of the house to let us in.

"No key," Stan said as he stood up. "I'm asking again, you okay with this?"

This was unlawful entry, what we were attempting to do. It was a no no for private investigators, and yet, we all did it. I had done it before and was arrested for it, because I had. Unfortunately for the police, they had to let me go because I exposed crucial evidence for them.

Not sure if we'd do that here, but we needed more information.

Stan jumped down the stoop, and I followed him around the side of the house. We took a narrow brick path hiding ourselves behind bushes, and most importantly out of the view of neighbors.

We climbed the deck and stood in front of the large sliding doors which overlooked a long narrow back yard. The yard was bordered on two sides with bushes, the third, a narrow clump of trees looked as though they had been here before the house was built. I only felt partially safe from prying eyes.

Stan and I searched for a key to get us through the single door to the laundry room. There was nothing in the grill, under cushions, or above the sliding doors.

When all else fails, use the lock picks. Stan pulled out his and knelt beside the door handle. I watched as he jiggled around in the lock until it popped opened.

We slipped on gloves and entered the house, closed and locked the door behind us.

My eyes scanned the small laundry room. It was dark, yet tidy and after taking a quick peek inside of the cabinets, I noticed Neal was clean and organized. But as I figured there wasn't anything worthy in the laundry room.

We crossed into a hallway that led to the kitchen and began to get to work, searching through piles of mail, opening cabinets and drawers.

I glanced in the canisters on the counter and in the pantry. "He's really organized," I said as my phone buzzed.

I glanced at the screen. It was Detective Clyde. "Crap. We don't have much time. They just got the warrant."

"You look for anything down here. I'll handle upstairs."

We separated at the stairs, and I looked around the front room. I started with the baskets on the shelves. Even the baskets were organized with playing cards, games, notebooks.

I opened more baskets and found pictures of family and friends, but nothing linking him to Janelle.

After looking through six baskets stored on the shelves, I knelt down besides the footlocker that Neal used for a coffee table. I cleared off the pile of decorative books, removed the candle and opened the lid. The locker contained photo albums, journals, framed pictures, and a box, surprisingly without a lock. I pulled it out and opened the lid.

Stan finished his preliminary of the bedrooms and saw me on the floor. “Find something?”

“Pictures and this…” I looked inside the box. “Crap. We need to go.”

Stan stood over me and looked inside the box. “Put everything back the way you found it, now.”

I closed the lid on the box that contained the gun, most likely the murder weapon, and put everything back in the box as I remembered. I closed the lid of the footlocker, put the decorative book over the void where there was no dust, and followed suit with the candle.

Stan stood at the window. “Now, Nikki. They’re here.”

I jumped up and took a final look at the room, hoping it was just as it was when we arrived. Car doors closed and footsteps walked up the path. We ran toward the back of the house to the laundry room as the doorbell rang. Stan looked out to the backyard.

"That way," Stan pointed and opened the door as the police pounded on the door. Stan, even in his 70s, was spry and jumped over the side of railing of the deck. I followed him down to the ground, a little deeper than I anticipated.

We were hidden behind bushes, up against the lattice at the base of the deck as two police officers stationed themselves at the back door.

It was chaos as the police busted through the front door. We could hear the footsteps pounding on the floor, voices barking orders.

With the officers standing watch, Stan and I crawled through the shrubbery and inside the clump of trees. I stood and limped as far from the house as I could.

Stan knelt down and watched the house from our hiding spot.

I slid my gloves off, shoved them in my pocket and took in the backyard and the neighbor's yard. "We can't get out of here until they're done."

Stan glanced around our location and nodded.

"Even if we head toward the street, we'll be caught," he said. "Leaving toward our left we'll have to walk past the house, we'll be seen. We can't run around the other way, through these yards because an owner can see us, and there's no cover. So yeah. Hunker down and watch. We may learn something."

I did as he suggested and leaned against a tree. With nothing currently going on outside, I pulled out my phone and searched for pictures of various guns to find out what Neal had stashed away in his footlocker.

"Your kids are going through something," Stan said as I thought I found the picture of Neal's gun.

"Yeah. I promise, I won't let that get in the way."

"It's not easy to work when you're a mom." His concentration hadn't been broken as he spoke to me. He was still watching.

"Do you have kids?"

I swear he shuddered when I asked. He didn't answer right away.

"I do. I wasn't a great father."

"Are you now?"

He chuckled. "I'd like to think I am."

"My kids are fighting. They're working on it. I think it's an indirect result of their horrible relationship with their father. But then, they are siblings, and that's pretty normal."

"Hopefully their father will figure it out and not take as long as it took me."

"He's learning. I'm sorry they were distracting."

"If you're out on your own, you'll need to be more careful. Tonight, you had me. If you didn't, you could have gotten caught breaking in."

"It's happened before. I wouldn't be surprised if it happens again."

Footsteps crossed the deck. I sat straighter and watched boxes being taken from the house.

"As long as you're my apprentice, you'll be more careful. I plan on teaching you the right way to do things."

"The right way to not get caught?" I asked.

Police were congregating at the stairs to the deck speaking loud enough we might be able to pick up some of what they were saying. I trained my phone toward them and recorded them.

"That's also illegal," Stan said as he watched them.

"You ever done it?"

He looked at me and grimaced.

I laughed and shut down the recorder, returning to the pictures of guns. I finally found it. Neal had a .38 special in his box. The same gun that killed Janelle. "He owns the type of gun Janelle was killed with. I found bullets in Janelle's safe that fit that gun."

"And the other guy, Marvin. He was killed by a?"

I had some notes on my phone and pulled them up. "He was killed with a colt."

"He might've done it. It looks like we can get out of here. Ready?"

"Yeah."

I was ready to go home, take a shower and climb into bed. I'd deal with the kids in the morning.

CHAPTER 21

I walked in, exhausted from the search and hiding as the police did their thing. I did feel guilty, but at least I knew Neal was probably Janelle's murderer.

"How did the stakeout go?" Will asked. He was watching tv with the kids and stood when I came in.

"Great. We may have learned something useful. So why are down here? I told you to separate. I can't have you texting me when I'm on stakeout."

I didn't want to have this conversation now since it was almost midnight.

"We're sorry, Mom. It happened," Jacob said.

"Multiple times. Multiple kids. When I'm on a stakeout, I need to be vigilant. What the hell happened? I thought you were working it out."

"We did. Marshall called. We talked for a while. Jacob got mad at that." Emily glared at Jacob.

"I shouldn't have. And I apologized."

"When I tell you I'm on a stakeout, there's two things. Don't tell anyone what I'm doing and don't call unless it's an absolute emergency." I couldn't hide the frustration in my voice.

"We're sorry, Mom. Really. We're good now. We promise."

"Apology accepted. I'm bushed and need to shower and go to sleep."

"Oh. Marshall called because the guy you asked him about. The one in Janelle's murder case contacted him. Marshall was a little spooked by it."

"Neal Enders contacted Marshall? There's no way he should have known who Marshall was. I never told him who. How did he…"

My brain and heart raced. How did he find out who fingered him from all those years ago?

"Is Marshall, okay? Did the guy hurt him at all?"

Emily shook her head. "No. He said it was creepy, and he was a little pissed when he called. I told him you wouldn't have told the guy. He found out some other way," Emily said.

"Call Marshall," I ordered.

Emily did. I took the phone. "Hi, Marshall. It's Mrs. Page. Are you okay?"

"Yeah. I'm fine. Emily said you didn't tell that guy. Is that true?"

"I didn't tell him. I don't know how he found out who you were. But I will find out. Did he threaten you or say anything?" I asked.

"He was creepy. He asked why I fingered him? I told him I didn't know what he was talking about. I didn't know who he was or why he was coming at me. Mrs. Page, what the hell's going on?"

"The only reason I asked if you knew him is because your name came up in my investigation. The only reason it mattered is because it highlighted a connection between two people in this case. A connection I didn't have before. I'm sorry for dragging you into this. He shouldn't have found you. What happened?"

"I musta convinced him I wasn't the guy he was looking for. He seemed angry, and it sounded like he mighta found someone else to hassle. He seemed a little frazzled, like he was high or something."

"I'm really sorry this happened. When did it happen?"

"Lunch time. He found me at work."

"I'm going to call the police detective in charge of the investigation and let him know. I'm very sorry about that."

"It's okay. A little weird but okay. He said something under his breath. Like he didn't think I could hear. He said your name. So, be careful, okay, Mrs. Page?"

"Thanks Marshall. Try and have a good night."

I dialed Clyde, he answered on the first ring. "Mrs. Page. I was going to call you in the morning."

"You were?"

"We found the murder weapon. What else can you tell me about Neal Enders?"

"Nothing much except I started to think about him as a suspect because of that link between Janelle and Dr. Hubble through that patient. The patient happened to recognize Neal. Which means he was around Janelle a lot back then. Neal found that patient. He shouldn't have been able to. I didn't tell him who recognized him. He went to that person's place of employment to ask him questions."

"Neal hasn't returned home. We're searching for him right now. When did he contact this former patient?"

"Lunch time. You have someone on the house still?"

"Yes. Neal's gone. We tracked him to dinner, a date it appears, but from there, we don't know. His date thought he was going home. You need to be careful."

I ran for my front window and looked outside. While it was dark outside, I could still see the protection detail across from my house. "Is the DEA still watching my house?"

"Yes," Clyde said. "I'll call them and make sure. You see someone outside?"

"Yes."

I was supposed to be careful. I thought I had been. How is this happening again?

I called Stan.

"Yeah. Nikki. Everything okay?"

"Neal Enders. He's missing. The police are looking for him. And he found the patient that linked Janelle and Dr. Hubble," I said so quickly I needed to catch my breath.

"DEA still watching the house?"

"Clyde's checking."

"Shit just happens to you, don't it?" he asked.

"I swear I was being careful. Not going after Sebastian having you with me. Letting you train me."

"Everything okay with your kids?"

I looked over. The kids were standing in the doorway between the kitchen and the dining room.

"They're fine. I'm not."

"They run when they know their secrets have been discovered. He's going to lash out. He's gonna try to fix it. If he calls, keep him talking. Figure out his plan."

"I'll do my best. I'll keep you posted."

I walked back to my family. Will put his arm around me. "So, we're in hypervigilant mode?" Will asked.

"Yes. If you have plans for tomorrow, cancel them. We'll hang out here. The police are looking for the suspect."

"And he's looking for you?" Jacob asked.

"He blames me for putting the police on him."

"Mom. You really are a trouble maker," Julia said.

"I'm sorry about that. I keep putting you into danger." It occurred to me there was still time to quit the program and go on with my life to something safe.

"I should quit investigating. It's not safe."

"And what will you do then? Go back to being a paralegal?" Jacob asked.

"I was good at it. My life was safe; our lives were safe. Ever since I started investigating things, my life has become dangerous. I've put you in danger too many times." I wiped a tear from my eyes.

"And besides, I was good at being a paralegal."

"But you're so good at getting to the truth and you solved that cold case," Emily said.

"We have a protection detail outside our house. You're in danger. I don't think I can do this any longer." I wiped away another tear.

"Mom. You can't give up your dreams. You like investigating. We're fine. They're watching the house. We feel safe," Julia said.

"I just told you to stay in all day tomorrow and not leave. That's not normal," I said.

"Mom. You need to do for you. We're safe. We have Will to keep us safe. Don't quit because it gets hard."

"You mean unsafe?"

"Just don't quit. Not tonight," Jacob said.

I reminded myself to not make any life changing decisions until I had a night of sleep. Maybe it would look better in the morning.

"It's late. Get ready for bed. Go to sleep. We'll see how things work out in the morning."

CHAPTER 22

I stared at my notes as I put the timeline together. Marvin was killed, then Janelle was killed and discovered first. George disappeared and then Marvin was discovered dead.

As Stan would ask, what does that tell us.

Originally, we assumed George ran because he thought he was next. We thought Sebastian had killed Janelle to scare someone and then we thought Marvin was killed first to scare Janelle.

Either way we thought Marvin and Janelle were killed because of the insurance fraud, because evidence led us to believe there were two killers.

But then the connection between Dr. Hubble and Janelle led me to Neal Enders, ex-boyfriend who probably killed Janelle because she didn't love him like he loved her.

So did Sebastian kill Marvin, and then Neal killed Janelle to make it look like the same killer? But how did Neal know about Marvin's murder before we did? We, meaning me and the police, didn't find out about it until after Janelle died?

I've been stuck on that question since the focus of Janelle's murder turned to Neal Enders and his disappearance. He hadn't been seen since Stan and I sat outside his house last night. It was now 4 p.m. the next day.

I opened my file for Janelle's murder and pulled out the phone records. Marvin died a week before Janelle. I circled all the phone calls from someone other than friends and family and co-workers and stared at a recurring incoming phone number. I had dialed the number; it went to a voice mail without a message. I hung up and hadn't found who the burner phone belonged to. After Marvin died, this phone number contacted Janelle, it was a fifteen-minute call. Did someone advise Janelle that Marvin was dead. Was it a threat to her? Was Neal there to hear the call or did she call him to tell him?

I looked at that day, a day in the life of Janelle, a frightened woman acting out, and making poor decisions. And there on that day she received a call from the mysterious caller, she called Neal. It was a short call, and I made a leap and thought maybe he came over to comfort a friend. How much did he know about what was going on with her?

I dialed his phone number on the off chance he really wasn't hiding and had come back home, or went into work, or was taking some vacation time. I was ready to leave a message, to tell Neal I wanted to speak with him about what happened the day Janelle found out Marvin was dead. I was shocked when the phone stopped ringing. If there was someone on the other end, they didn't greet me.

"Neal. It's Nikki Page. I need to speak to you. Are you okay? People are looking for you," I said quickly.

"Don't call this number again," a sultry female voice said.

I was too stunned at first to speak. "I'm sorry, I'm looking for Neal Enders. Is he available?" I finally found my words.

"Neal's not here. Don't call this number again," the voice said again. This time it was terse and to the point.

"Again. I'm sorry. I'm just looking for a friend. I must have the wrong number."

I hung up the phone before she could say anything else. But now a stranger had my number and could search and possibly find where I was.

Another reason to not pursue a PI license.

I ran for the window. My protectors were still outside and would be until it was time to switch shifts at seven. I shuddered and texted Detective Clyde.

I told him about the call to Janelle, the day Marvin was murdered, and her call to Neal Enders the same day. I explained why I was stuck on that point. How did Neal know about Marvin's murder? It seemed it was there in the phone records. At least I could presume it was.

I waited for him to text me back, but that might take time especially if they were chasing a lead. When he didn't reply, I texted again and had let him know a strange woman answered Neal Enders's phone.

There was nothing left for me to do except to wait until Neal Enders, George Egan, or Sebastian was found.

All I could do was wait.

***

I was so lost in those thoughts as I cleaned my kitchen. When the doorbell rang, I jumped.

The kids were in the basement, heeding my advice to not leave the house today. Maybe it was a friend. But at nine at night?

I glanced outside the dining room window. In the artificial light beside the door, stood a very stylish woman on my stoop. Probably 5'9", slim, in black slacks and a tan leather jacket. Her hair was in a messy, yet sophisticated bun, her lips bright red. And here I was in leggings, a large T-shirt and just enough make up to not look sickly.

I glanced at the car belonging to the night crew watching the house. One of the agents exited the car.

I answered the door. She looked down at me, her lips pursed as though I was less than. Who was this woman?

"Mrs. Page?"

"How can I help you?" I asked. I stared at her perfect skin, well put together makeup, and her face became more familiar.

Where have I seen her before?

"We have a friend in common," she said in that low, slow way she had over Neal's phone.

In an instant, her face was on a picture, one that I had found on Janelle's USB drive that her lawyer had given me after she died.

"Katrina Winston?" I asked the woman.

She smiled a dazzling white smile.

"I was so looking forward to revealing that. And there you go, ruining that for me." Her smile widened. "May I come in?"

"No." I said. I could hear the movie wafting from the basement and the floor vibrating with the loud music during an action scene.

I also could see the shadow moving closer to the house.

"If you'd like to play it that way. Okay. So, tell me then, why did you call Neal Enders?" she asked as though this was a regular conversation between friends.

"It was a wrong number. I told the voice on the phone," I said.

Katrina Winston tried to keep her composure. She bit her lip, her hands shook.

"You were looking for Neal. Why?" she asked again.

"He's a witness in a murder case I'm investigating. I wanted to ask him further questions."

"Well don't. Leave it to the police."

Footsteps came closer to us, as two men were walking up my driveway. Katrina Winston heard the steps and looked at them. Without missing a beat, she turned and walked away, back down the path to the driveway to her car. In the dark, all I could tell was the car was a sports car, and it looked black. She started the car and peeled out of the driveway.

When the two agents reached my door, they stopped. "Who was that?"

"Katrina Winston."

The taller of the two agents immediately reached for his phone and made a call.

Katrina had sped backward down the driveway and slammed down on the gas pedal. Her tires squealed and when she regained control, she shot down the street. It didn't take long before I no longer saw her taillights.

"Did she threaten you?" the shorter of the two men asked. His name, if I remember correctly, was Jeff. The other, I couldn't remember.

"Not really. I had called Neal Enders to ask him some questions. She answered his phone, and I suppose once she figured out where I lived, she came here to tell me to stop calling him."

I folded my arms against my chest, a visual message to them to leave me alone. They weren't leaving yet.

"Is there something else?" I asked.

"Neal Enders was arrested about an hour ago," Jeff said.

"Katrina didn't say. I wonder if she knows," I said.

"We shouldn't have to tell you this, but be careful. We don't know anything about her except that she has been with Sebastian for years," no name said.

"You don't know her role in the organization, or why she knows Neal Enders and what role she had in Janelle's death."

My phone buzzed. It was a text message from Detective Clyde.

Interesting. Thank you and Neal was arrested. His gun matched the bullet that killed Janelle.

I breathed a sigh of relief. "You knew the bullet matched Neal Enders' gun," I said.

"We assumed with the arrest. We'll be here until morning. In the meantime, we'll let the others know to lock down where Neal's phone has been to find where Katrina lives," Jeff said.

I nodded.

"If she calls again, let us know."

"Thank you. I appreciate knowing you're out there."

A car drove down the street and without streetlights, I only realized it was Will when the car pulled into the driveway.

"It's Will," I said when both men tensed. They relaxed momentarily and headed back toward their cars, walking through the grass to get across the street.

Rather than entering the garage, Will came down the brick pathway to the front door, jogging to reach me.

"What happened?" he asked before he climbed the stoop.

"I met Katrina Winston about twenty minutes ago. They were checking on me," I said and pointed to the boys.

"She found you? How?"

He put his arms around me. I felt myself tremble against him. He walked me inside.

I explained my question, and my attempt to get it answered by Neal and how Katrina answered the phone.

"How does she know Neal?"

I shrugged.

"That's a good question. I'd like that answer myself. Oh. And Neal's been arrested in Janelle's murder. He's at the police station now."

"The gun matched," he said as he rubbed the stubble on his chin.

He sat me down at the kitchen table. I was still trembling as Will heated up the water and made me a cup of tea.

The movie was over, and the kids clomped up the stairs.

"You okay, Mom?" Jacob asked.

"I'm fine. We have an arrest in Janelle's murder. I think I'm just emotional. Nothing to worry about." I was trying to be normal, light, and relieved.

"That's great. Who was it?" Emily asked.

"An ex-boyfriend named Neal. Marshall actually helped me find the connection. Is he okay after Neal came after him?"

Emily shrugged. "I haven't talked to him. I'm done with him. I'm rooming with Susannah next year. Lisa and Shelby think I'm wrong. That I'm making a bigger issue than it was." Her eyes filled with tears.

"I'm sorry," I said and stood beside her, my arms wrapped around her. "I think this is a good thing. They broke your trust. They might make it up to you in the future or not. But you need to do what's best for you." I held her tighter. It took my mind off of my own shaky emotions.

She pulled away. "I'll be okay. Susannah is excited. She didn't want to be with her roommate anyway. It'll be fine." She wiped away tears.

Julia pulled on her sleeve. "Let's watch that other show upstairs."

Julia then turned to me and put her arms around me. "Proud of you, Mom. You're gonna be a great PI." She kissed my cheek. All grown up.

I wanted to cry.

They walked away, upstairs to Emily's room and her tv.

"You guys, okay?" I asked Jacob.

"Yeah. They're gonna watch Outlander or something." He rolled his eyes. "The game's on." Jacob addressed Will.

Will handed me a tea. "Sure. In a sec."

Jacob retreated to the den. Will stood beside me. "We can go upstairs and talk if you'd like."

I shook my head. "No. I'm good. I need to let Stan know what's happened and write up the final report. Technically it goes to you."

Will chuckled. "I can do without it. You sure Stan can't wait?"

I shook my head again. "You watch. It's the late game, and I'll come and sit with you when I'm done."

Will kissed my cheek and headed to the sofa with Jacob.

I went to my room, closed the door and dialed Stan.

"Nikki. What's the word?" Stan said. He was slowly warming up to me, getting less formal, much more casual.

I told him about my theory about Neal and my call to him, his arrest, and meeting Katrina Winston.

"Really? Your bodyguards still out there?"

"They're still out there. I'm concerned about Neal's connection to Katrina and the whole plan."

"There might not be. She's been silent in the scheme but might be a big player. She might only know about Neal because of Janelle's death. He killed one of the operatives in the plan. She might be going after him."

"Again, I'm nervous about the link. He could be in danger."

"Not if he's in jail. They won't post bail until tomorrow. Court's not open."

Good point.

"For tonight, he's safe," I said.

"Good work, Nikki. You pulled it on home. You're very good at what you do."

I was suddenly as embarrassed as I was tired. It had been a stressful two weeks.

In that moment, I just didn't realize it was far from over.

CHAPTER 23

With the police finishing up with Janelle's murder and finding out who killed Marvin, I was back to background checks for Stan. I was good with that.

Detective Clyde called me as I was running a check on a man named Chester Linn.

"Hi, Detective. How can I help you?" I said as I printed off my first run.

"I have news."

"I'm listening," I said as I leaned back in the desk chair.

"We believe we have the cottage where the pictures of George Egan were shot. We found the blood pool, the room set up to look as though there was a struggle. Some other documents and evidence used to imply it was George in those pictures. And it could very well have been but there was no body. We searched the forest near the house, all through the house. Either he was killed and was moved and buried somewhere else, or the murder was fake."

"We thought he might have faked his death."

"It looks like it might have been. I have a favor to ask." He sounded serious and after everything, I was surprised he wanted my help.

"Sure," I said.

"The blood we found at the scene belonged to a man named Dennis Perkins. Do you know that name?"

"Oh." Well, forget my theories. But who is Dennis Perkins?

"Do you know who that is?" he asked.

I traveled back through the case but wasn't able to pinpoint the name.

"I can't think of who that is right now, but I can go through my files and see if his name comes up."

"That would be good. And uh… there's something else."

I held my breath as he paused.

"Katrina Winston paid Neal Enders's bail."

"Oh," I said quietly. I wasn't sure what else to say, and I couldn't figure out what was going on between them.

"Do you know of any connection between the two of them?" he asked.

"No. I can't think of a connection unless she's gonna do

something to him because he killed Janelle, and she was the scheme's best operative."

"That's what we're thinking as well," he said plainly.

"What favor did you have for me besides looking for Dennis Perkins in my notes?" I asked since we had gone so far off the path.

"Oh, yes. I was hoping you could dig up something about Dennis Perkins. There are no missing person reports for him. It's as if he doesn't exist."

I smiled to myself. "I can do that. I'll have something for you as soon as I find it. By the way, did you ever find where Katrina called me from?"

"Yes. She lives in Long Grove. But no one is there now. And Neal Enders never arrived home after being released from jail. We think they both disappeared. We tried them at Sebastian's home, but no one answered. We think because the prime suspects in three murders are missing, we can get court orders for Katrina and Sebastian's house now. I'll call you when we do, and you can watch."

"Thanks. I'll check on that name and get back to you. And thank you for including me on the search."

"You've given us some good leads. We think you can help. Let me know what you find out."

He hung up abruptly, but I was getting used to it.

I returned to my work for Stan.

It took me another forty minutes to go through the list of names, finding the data we were after. When I finished, I typed up my notes and sent Stan the initial information.

It was time to search Janelle's murder file. I went through each piece of evidence that Janelle had left for me. It came to me as I reviewed the insurance claims. Dennis Perkins. He was an insurance adjuster. Huh?

I continued to dig through the internet, all my favorite databases and websites. There was nothing on Dennis Perkins after 1975 when he graduated college until he resurfaced five years ago when he started working for Adams Medical.

Searching a little further, I found more information about Dennis Perkins and found his college graduation picture in a newspaper from downstate Illinois. I enlarged the picture and stared at the face. I pulled out a picture of George Egan. Dennis Perkins could have been his son.

Dennis Perkins, what did you do in 1975 that made you up and disappear to become George Egan?

Was I correct?

I pulled up George Egan and travelled backward though his life. When I had checked on him previously, I found what I needed as it applied to Janelle's murder and hadn't gone back farther. What I found weird was George Egan hadn't appeared until 1977 when he graduated with a masters in speech therapy. But there was no undergraduate degree or personal data. He didn't exist until then.

"How did no one check his background?" I asked myself.

Now I had two people who changed their names.

I looked at the information that linked Sebastian Cole and Dr. Hubble. Jacob had found it in an old legal filing. And there it was, a listing of all of the employees who worked for Dr. Hubble. Dennis Perkins had worked for him too.

Sebastian Cole had found himself with legal problems; was that the same for Dennis Perkins?

Yes. He was wanted for rape of a young woman. He had been convicted and headed to jail. Was that when Dr. Hubble stepped in to help him?

Dr. Hubble, the savior to the convicts, saving them from jail, changing their names, giving them a new life. A new life of crime, however.

Is this possible?

I texted as much as I could to Detective Clyde.

He gave me no other information. I figured things were getting heavy and moving quickly. Eventually, he called me instead.

***

Stan met me at Katrina's house. A large six-bedroom, eight-bathroom home, with impeccable landscaping in a high-end neighborhood.

The inside of the house was just as well put together. White walls, a black and white marble floor in an entry foyer about half the size of my downstairs. Gold statues, a large floral bouquet on a center table in the middle of the foyer, a large winding staircase to the second floor. It wasn't jealousy that made me go "Wow." It was the fact we couldn't find her anywhere online and yet she had money to buy or rent this house.

I was given gloves and sent on my way, concentrating on the living area off the kitchen.

Two bookshelves were set on either side of the fireplace. They were filled with books and picture frames. On second glance, the pictures in the frames were what the frames came with. There were no personal tchotchkes or pictures of friends and family.

"It doesn't look lived in," I said as I pulled down one of the books and shuffled through the pages.

"It really doesn't," Stan said as he took the bookshelf to the left. I continued through the decorative books finding each of them to be regular, weirdly titled books. Nothing else.

I opened the cabinets below the shelves. They were empty. I stood and looked around the room. Across in the kitchen, the crime scene investigators opened and closed cabinets and drawers, even the refrigerator.

"This is where Katrina called from?" I asked as I glanced around the pristine room.

"Yes," Detective Clyde said from behind me.

"There's hardly any food in the cabinets or refrigerator, and there's nothing personal in the house. Do we think this is a ruse?" I asked.

"We'll see when they've checked the upstairs," Clyde said and turned to the stairs. The officers in charge were bringing down very little in their bags.

The CSI shook her head when she came down the stairs. "There's not much here. We've even taken to looking for hidden holes in the walls."

"And the basement?" I asked.

As I said that, the basement door squeaked open. Several investigators came upstairs with boxes. They plopped them on the sofa and opened them.

Inside was a surprise, yet not one. The boxes contained survival gear, knives, extra water, freeze dried foods and other essentials.

"She used this house as a safe house. Expensive safe house," I said.

"It keeps up appearances," Clyde said.

It still made no sense to me, but I supposed it could be a logical explanation. It didn't sit well with me.

"Has anyone found Neal Enders?" I asked.

"He's in the wind so to speak. He is expected in court in four weeks. If we don't find him by then, we can convict in abstention. It's not ideal but we can do it. We're still looking," Clyde said.

I walked to the large windows on the back wall that overlooked the yard. The five thousand square foot house sat on a little over an acre.

The yard was surrounded by bushes and flowers, a lovely trail creating coziness in an otherwise sterile environment.

At the back of the property line, was a small shed. I was surprised, usually those weren't permitted in neighborhoods like this.

"Anyone check out the shed back there?" I asked without turning around. Stan joined me at the window.

"We discovered something in the basement," said an investigator.

We both turned, and they waved us downstairs.

"It will be answered now, I think," Clyde said.

We followed the investigators into the basement. It was huge, as wide as the house and as long.

Toward the back facing the back yard was a door that had been hidden by paneling. On the other side of the paneling was a passageway that led to a tunnel under the backyard.

"Think that goes to the shed?" I asked Stan.

He smiled. "Probably."

It was a straight passage, well-engineered with beams to support the weight of ground above us. There was something else, several doors off the corridor. With my hands still gloved I turned one of the knobs. Stan stopped and joined me. There was a bunk bed. Unmade, empty food containers. One of the investigators joined us.

"I'll take the lead," he said and walked past us. We searched under the mattresses and in the dirty bedding that hadn't been changed in years.

"It stinks in here," I said when I stood.

"It's been used. Not cleaned," the investigator said.

Stan was still looking through the mattress on the top bunk. "Here," he said and pulled out a bag of pills. "Wonder if the mules come by the house, get their product, and stay the night before leaving?" he said.

"How did she build this? This is incredible and creepy all at the same time," I said.

"We think the drug trade of this operation has been going on for decades. They changed over to the prescription drugs and then moved into insurance fraud," the investigator said as he put the drugs into an evidence bag.

"No word on Sebastian?" I asked.

"Not yet. And no sign of George," the investigator said.

"Search for Dennis Perkins instead," I advised.

He looked at me. "We heard something about that. I think it's already being done."

We left the room and followed the others down the tunnel.

Detective Clyde was at the end of the tunnel beside a ladder leading to what I thought was the shed. When we arrived, he turned and looked at us. "Find something?" he asked.

"Prescription drugs," the investigator said and held up the package.

Clyde nodded. "They've found supplies hidden inside planters. They've found packaging, travel bags in the storage units."

"Small part of the drug trafficking," Stan said.

"We're guessing there're other houses throughout the suburbs, across the country. Small, less noticeable, easy to hide. We'll send a canvas around the neighborhood, see if anyone saw odd cars at odd hours. The usual drill," Clyde said.

"My simple investigation turned into a huge case," I murmured.

"Sometimes that happens," Stan said.

My phone buzzed and I was worried it was one of the kids. This was bad timing. It wasn't.

"Oh shit." I held up my phone. I received a text from an unknown number with a picture of a kidnapped Neal Enders and a message warning me he didn't have much time.

***

The police took control of my phone and asked the kidnapper what they wanted. I was ordered to wait for instructions.

While we waited, the team began to triangulate where that text had come from.

Because the phone hadn't belonged to a specified person, and was most likely a burner phone, we couldn't guarantee the phone, and the caller were in the same place.

Stan and I left the house and drove to the police station while a team remained behind to continue the search. I was sequestered in a conference room with Stan, a computer, and my phone. I contacted the kids, and Will and let them know it would be a while before I got home.

An hour after I called Will, he showed up at the police station.

"You don't know where he is?" Will asked when he sat. He had brought coffee, donuts, and bagels.

"They tried to track where the text had come from, but it's a burner. They have a team checking it out now," I said.

"Do they know who took him?"

"Katrina paid his bail and then took him," Stan said as he looked through the donuts.

"She finally made an appearance." Will sighed and leaned back in his chair.

"What do you know about her, Mr. Mann?" Detective Clyde asked.

Will shrugged and shook his head. "I met her in St. Thomas when we met Sebastian. They claimed they were married. We had no reason not to believe them. But something happened between Janelle and Sebastian during that trip. I had no idea what and my marriage suffered as a result."

"She didn't talk about what she did for a living or her interests?"

"Nothing. Sebastian told us he was a speech therapist and where he worked. Nikki later discovered he had worked for Dr. Hubble, and he knew Janelle back in the day. Janelle didn't give a sign she knew him."

"Your wife had big secrets," Clyde said.

"She did," Will agreed.

"We haven't pinpointed who Katrina really is. We still have investigators looking for clues to her identity," Clyde said.

"Did you check on Katrina Cole or Sebastian Cole? He changed his name," I reminded Clyde.

He nodded. "I'll have them check for Katrina Cole. We did look for Sebastian Cole and found nothing in the last ten years. Everything was prior to that."

Clyde sent a text. "We found security video of Sebastian leaving through O'Hare airport. He left two days ago and from what we could tell he left for San Francisco. The police there finally located him. They're surveilling him and will let us know when he leaves, and we can watch the airport for him."

"He's still alive. Any word on George Egan, or I guess, Dennis Perkins?" I asked.

"I want to bring Madeline Egan in for a formal interview. I'd like you, Nikki, inside. See if we can appeal to her sense of protecting her husband and get her to tell us where he is, since we know those pictures aren't George Egan or I guess Dennis Perkins," Clyde said.

"I wonder if she knows he changed his name to escape his rape conviction," I said.

"We went to tell her that we think he's still alive. We also let her know about that. She wasn't relieved," Clyde said.

"It doesn't mean she did something to him. We just ruined his plan," I said.

Will held on to my hand as I took a sip of my coffee. We were circling onto something. We just needed to find Neal and figure out who killed Marvin. We had the why for Janelle, but not for him.

"Do you have the police files for Marvin Gartner's murder?" I asked.

Detective Clyde nodded, walking from the room. We still weren't alone; there were several officers waiting for word about Katrina.

I glanced at my phone when it buzzed. It was the kids. Will texted them from his phone telling them to call or text him. He'd get word to me. I glanced at him, offered half a smile and sighed.

Detective Clyde returned with a box, set it on the table and pulled the lid. He found the folder and passed it to me.

I looked inside. I found the evidence Marvin had on the syndicate and reviewed the notes. "Marvin was killed first. Why?" I said out loud but returned to the notes, searching for anything that I hadn't seen in Janelle's folders. "Can you get me what you had from Janelle's folders? Please," I asked as I continued to scan the documents.

I compared Janelle's evidence to Marvin's. It appeared to be all the same, like she was working with him. Why was Marvin killed?

"It made sense that Janelle was killed because someone found out she was working with the FBI. But if Neal did it for a completely different reason and no one knew she was going to the FBI, I still can't figure out Marvin. The why. He sounded like he really liked Janelle, that he was a nice man, quiet."

"But he was deep in the insurance fraud," Stan said.

He was. I returned to the documents.

"Is there anything else you found in his house that's not here?" I asked. It was all the same, everything I had gotten from Janelle. I couldn't see why he'd be murdered.

"What are you looking for?" Clyde asked as he returned to the evidence box.

"I don't know. Something to tell me he was killed because he knew something or threatened something." I whined it out. I was tired and crabby. I glanced at my phone. Still nothing from Katrina and no word on where she and Neal might be.

Clyde searched inside and found another folder from the FBI. "Try this," he said.

I opened a yellowish folder and dumped the contents on the table. It was more of the same, more of what Janelle had given Marvin to hold. But stuck to a page in the middle of a pile of copies of claim forms was an envelope. I pulled the open envelope from the claim form.

Inside was a letter from Marvin to Jackson Beale regarding Dennis Perkins. He was telling the FBI about the insurance fraud, and he was coming forward because he couldn't take it any longer.

Marvin was the whistleblower? What was Janelle?

I went back through the letters from Janelle to Jackson Beale and from Jackson to Janelle. There was a similar letter from Janelle to Jackson about the fraud; it was dated after Marvin's letter to Jackson. And Janelle took over the process. Was Marvin too shy or worried or scared?

I was about to call Jackson Beale for answers, but instead, I got a text message.

My hand shook when I scrolled through my phone and read the message. I handed the phone to Detective Clyde.

He made a call, and the troops assembled.

"She wants me there alone," I said.

Will squeezed my hand.

"I know Mrs. Page. But you know that's not gonna happen."

We left the table covered in evidence, but one of the officers collected what I had been doing. I followed Detective Clyde. Will and Stan walked on either side of me as if they could be the ones to protect me from Katrina as we headed out to meet her.

CHAPTER 24

"This is not standard operating procedure," Detective Clyde groused as he drove us north of Chicago, heading toward Wisconsin. Will and I sat in the back seat, his hand firmly holding mine while Stan sat in the front beside the detective. It clearly wasn't standard operating procedure.

"She requested me," I reminded him, though I really didn't have to remind him. Detective Clyde was well aware Katrina was expecting to see me and his only option was to find out where Neal Enders was being stashed and if he was still alive.

"The only thing you'll be doing is showing your face. From a safe distance," Detective Clyde said.

"And if that's not enough?" Will asked. He squeezed my hand tighter; I thought I'd lose circulation in my hand.

"We know what we're doing. Mrs. Page is only there to show her face. Once Katrina sees her, she'll be taken away. We'll keep a close eye on you, Mrs. Page."

"Like the FBI did for Marvin and Janelle?" Will groused. He clearly hated this plan.

We continued north where houses and buildings became fewer and farther between as thick trees and evergreens lined the highway.

We were all quiet but the sound of the radio issued orders and plan discussions.

My name came up several times. Each time, Will's jaw clenched and he held my hand tighter.

We crossed into Wisconsin.

"What did you learn back at the police station?" Will asked.

Detective Clyde looked into the rearview mirror.

"Marvin contacted the FBI first. Once Janelle got involved, it seems like she took over for him."

"He liked her. He could have known she was in danger and went on her behalf," Will suggested.

"Then he could have been killed because they knew he went to the FBI," I said.

I leaned back and closed my eyes. I thought of the few times I've been on police stakeouts or at a police raid, picking up the offender. It was scary, nerve wracking and that was with me being on the outside looking in. Now I had to go in.

Katrina had to see me. Her message clearly stated she had something to say to me. I couldn't imagine what that could be, except to taunt me over the death of Janelle and possibly Neal.

I shuddered, and Will put his arm around me.

Detective Clyde pulled down a dirt road and followed the winding curves toward a farm. This location was more of what I expected for a drug den, mostly because it was out of the sight of neighbors, hidden in the trees, and most importantly, in the middle of nowhere.

Several cars stopped far enough away from the house, but still within sight.

"Stay here," Clyde ordered. I wasn't planning on leaving at all if I didn't have to.

He opened the door and stood behind it.

"Katrina Winston, police. Come out with Neal Enders, now!" he shouted through a bullhorn.

A gunshot rang out in the air, echoing across the trees. Clyde ducked behind the door.

"I want to see Nikki Page, now!" shouted Katrina.

"Come out without your gun, and we can make that happen!" shouted Clyde.

"I want to see her now!"

“She’s in the back of the car, and she’s not coming out until we see you out here. Your hands in the air, now!” Clyde said.

Officers and detectives secured positions behind their car doors, guns pointing to the front door, their eyes trained on the front door waiting for Katrina to exit.

I could barely breathe as the minutes ticked away.

Stan looked back at me. “You really have a way about the cases don’t you,” he said and winked at me. I grimaced as my stomach roiled.

***

Twenty minutes later, Neal Enders walked outside with his hands in the air.

“I didn’t do it! I didn’t kill Janelle! Katrina did it! She framed me! She ran out back! I’m innocent. Nikki, I didn’t do it!” he screeched as the police, including Detective Clyde rushed him. One of the officers kicked behind his knees forcing him to the ground. Another team rushed around the back in search of Katrina.

I watched with some relief and satisfaction as Neal was handcuffed.

“Did you know ‘im?” Stan asked Will.

“Neal? Not well. He was at our wedding, and was an old friend of Janelle’s. He was always cold, almost hostile toward me. I think it wore on Janelle, and she finally stopped seeing him. I was surprised she started dating him again, and he agreed to it." Will didn't sound bitter or angry. He sounded resigned to everything.

The scene unfolded as Detective Clyde pulled Neal to standing and patted him down. They had a conversation I couldn't hear, but based on their actions, Clyde was talking to him sternly, and Neal was pleading.

When the conversation was deemed over, Neal was led to a separate car and pushed inside.

I finally breathed a sigh of relief. "It could have gone worse," I said.

"I'll take this as a win. Let them find Katrina," Will said.

Police officers and investigative teams crisscrossed the yard and in and out of the house searching for evidence.

Detective Clyde joined us.

"I'm taking you back with us. They have it under control here, and based on the hostage situation, they can go in and collect evidence for that crime. It's getting late, and we want to deal with Neal Enders now."

He said nothing else as he started the car, and we followed Neal Enders back to the police station.

***

The police station was warm, or it was just exhaustion from dealing with Katrina and Neal all day. As I leaned back on the hard chair, Will kept the kids apprised of the latest. I closed my eyes and listened to the sounds of Stan searching through the files to have something to do as we waited for any police officer to update us on the search, and more importantly, tell us why we were still here.

From inside the closed conference room, I could hear shouting and could easily make out Detective Clyde and a very frantic Neal Enders.

While Neal claimed he was set up, and didn't do anything because he was innocent, I could make out my name. Without warning, something heavy was thrown into the door. The door bounced and shook against the weight. I feared it was Neal being thrown against it.

***

But Neal hadn't exactly been thrown into the door. It was him being restrained by the police officer when he lashed out and attacked the officer.

I almost believed he hadn't killed Janelle, almost.

When I entered the interrogation room, he sat there defeated, a bruise on his left cheek and holding his left arm where he crashed into the door while being restrained.

The officer held an icepack to his chin, where Neal had punched him.

What a mess.

Neal had asked for me. I was curious why, but I wasn't going to initiate the conversation. I felt exposed and vulnerable as I sat in the empty metal chair as the officers watched me.

"I didn't do it," he growled as he stared at the table.

"The gun," I said.

"It's not mine!" he shouted.

I placed the file on the table and shuffled through the documents and pictures. I finally found the gun report and slid it to him like I've seen the police do before.

Neal refused to look at it.

"The gun is registered to you. It's the gun used to kill Janelle. The gun was found in your house," I said.

He looked at the door. I saw the tears flow from his eyes.

Again, I refused to engage. This wasn't my job.

"I didn't kill her," Neal reiterated.

"She was killed with your gun," I reminded him.

"I didn't…" He wiped his cheeks.

"What happened the day she died?" I asked, my voice rising.

"I was so in love with her," he said, his voice cracked.

I watched him work through his memories or his story. He had known her over thirty years.

"She didn't love me. I wasn't good enough. First it was that guy in college; she dropped me for him. And then Will," he sneered.

“Why did you start dating her again? After what she did to you in college?” I asked.

“I loved her,” he growled.

“But she clearly wasn’t in love with you. She wasn’t even nice to you.”

His demeanor changed; his face was red with anger. “She was confused. She loved me. I just wasn’t enough. She had big needs.”

“She didn’t love you. She treated you like shit. Didn’t she tell you, you didn’t make enough money, or dress well enough? She was using you,” I said calmly.

“She wasn’t. She loved me. I know she loved me.” He pounded on the table, the handcuffs clinking together.

“Neal. Really? She cheated on you in college. She used you and cheated on you in this current relationship. She was using you. Can’t you see that?” I asked.

I wondered when Detective Clyde was going to join us. I wasn’t sure if I could keep this up. Neal wasn’t budging, and I wasn’t sure where to go with the questioning. We had the evidence against him.

“No!” he screeched. “That’s not…” he stood. The police officer by the door walked closer and looked at Neal.

“Sit down,” the guard said.

Neal sat quickly. He moved his hands to his lap and stared at them.

"You did it, Neal. You killed Janelle because she didn't love you. I saw the pictures. I saw your social media posts. She didn't even acknowledge you on her page. Ever."

Neal pounded the table again. His eyes widened. He stood again and bent forward until his face was inches from mine. His mouth puckered.

"You don't know. You weren't there. She was horrible. Selfish." His face was puffy and red. His pulse beat wildly against his neck.

"You killed her," I said quietly.

"I… I didn't mean to. It just happened."

He was still standing. I stood to face him.

"What happened?" I asked.

He hung his head. "She called me. She was never gonna get away from them. I asked her what she meant. That's when she told me everything. That she was in an insurance fraud scam and she wanted out and tried to get out but they killed Marvin Gartner. I tried to help her. I went over there to console her. But she got weird. Blamed me. Told me I couldn't help her. I told her I loved her, and we'd work it out. I'd help her. Get a lawyer. Go to the FBI."

Exhaustion wiped him out, and he slumped against the chair. "She told me no. She told me she was already working on it. They couldn't help her now. I tried. I really tried. But she turned on me. She blamed me for everything. If I had been a better, more supportive boyfriend, she wouldn't have gotten messed up in this. She just laid into me. I couldn't handle it anymore.

The morning she died, she called me hysterical. I was the only one who could help her. She needed my gun. She needed help killing someone. But I was sick of her using me, and that was too much. I told her no. She called me useless, worthless, waste of skin. I… I don't remember getting the gun and driving to see her. It was such a blur. But I had to tell her I was done. I couldn't deal with her anymore, and she wasn't gonna walk all over me again."

"What happened when you got there?"

The police officer left his spot by the door, and Detective Clyde walked in. He stayed by the door for the rest of the story even though he had been watching through the one-way mirror, and this was all being recorded.

I finally breathed a sigh of relief when I saw him.

"She was so happy to see me. I had the gun. I asked her for proof before I gave her the gun. She showed me her files. I believed she was in trouble and she asked me for the gun. I still didn't think I should give it to her so she reached for it. I told her no. She couldn't have it. I wasn't going to help her. She screamed at me. Same stuff I don't remember, except she lunged toward me, and the gun went off. I panicked. I left her on the floor and I ran."

"You didn't call 911 after you shot her?" Detective Clyde asked.

Neal was startled by his presence. "No," he said.

"The woman you love, as you say, was accidentally killed and you left her there to die?" Detective Clyde asked.

That didn't sound right. I went for the folder, but Clyde shook his head. I dropped my hands in my lap.

"It was an accident," Neal insisted. "There was blood all over and she was already dead when I left."

Detective Clyde walked to the table, yanked up the folder and searched for the autopsy report.

He pulled it out. "She was shot with a gun, your gun, clean through her heart. Care to change your story?" he asked.

"No. It was an accident. I didn't mean to kill her. The gun just went off." His voice was monotone. All the emotion gone, his will to survive seemed to leave his body. He was done with her.

CHAPTER 25

The long day ended with a short night. I woke up when Will woke up and made coffee and some breakfast. I sat beside him while he ate. It was the first time in what felt like days I had seen him.

"It's not completely over yet, is it?" he asked as he sipped his coffee.

"I'm done, I think. They're still looking for George Egan, Sebastian and Katrina Winston. From what the police told me last night; they also have a search warrant for Dr. Hubble's office and home. He seemed to have started this whole organization."

"Fifteen years ago?"

"It looks like he started putting the pieces together back then," I said.

"What's next?" He packed a folder in his bag.

"More research. Stan's sending over more work he hasn't gotten to yet because of Janelle's murder."

"So, you're staying a PI?" he asked.

"I don't know."

"Until you figure that out, how about going out to dinner tonight?" he asked.

"Hmmm. A date. That'd be good. We haven't done that in a while. The kids are settling down for the end of summer, and things are quieting down. That should be good."

"I've gotta run. I'll see you tonight." He kissed me, grabbed his bag and headed out. Things were feeling back to normal, and I was ready to get on with the next chapter.

By lunch, the kids were out of the house shopping for school supplies, and I was up to my eyebrows in work for Stan. I hadn't expected the phone call I got.

"This is Nikki," I said without reading my screen.

"Mrs. Page. Oh, Mrs. Page. I need your help," a scared high-pitched voice said. One that I didn't recognize at first.

"I'm sorry, who is this?" I asked.

"This is Madeline. Madeline Egan. I need your help," she pleaded.

"Mrs. Egan. What's the matter? Are you okay?"

She sounded panicked. I could imagine many reasons why, and they all worried me.

"George. He's back. He's injured, and I don't know what to do," she screeched.

The police figured he was still alive, hiding and faking his death to remain out of the view of Katrina and Sebastian and the police, for that matter.

"If he's injured get him to the hospital, and you must call the police. They've been looking for him," I implored but expected she wouldn't.

"No. Please, come. I need you here."

"Ok. I'm on my way."

I hung up. It was the last thing I wanted to be doing. As I put my items in neat piles and grabbed my bags, the kids entered with bags of their own and all the supplies they'd need for school.

"Where you going?" Jacob asked.

"I just received a call from a suspect's wife. I'll be out for a bit," I told them.

"I thought you were done with the case. Janelle's killer was arrested," Emily said as she took out snacks and chips from one of the many bags.

"All true. But there's still an unsolved murder. Her husband is a possible suspect. I promise I won't be too long."

"You better not be late. We're making dinner tonight," Julia said.

"Oh. I have a date tonight. Can we do it tomorrow?" I asked.

"A date. Oooh," Julia responded.

"Go put your things away and do something fun."

I headed out to George Egan's house to see what he had to say.

***

"Oh, thank goodness, Mrs. Page." A harried Madeline Egan let me inside. I followed her down a hallway and down a short staircase to a den. Standing at the sliding door was a man I assumed was George Egan. He had been missing over a week but looked like he had been held prisoner for a year. His collared shirt hung off his frame and was stained on the arms, frayed at the hem. His pants were ripped in the left knee.

His sunken eyes followed the sound of my footsteps, and he stared right through me as if not fully processing I was here.

"George, dear. This is Nikki Page. She's been looking for you. She can help."

Madeline smiled, but it felt forced. She was scared. I could read it on her face and see it in her trembling body.

"Everyone's been looking for you," I said.

He nodded but still didn't seem to process.

"Where have you been, George?"

He cleared his throat and tried to speak; words didn't

come out.

Madeline reached for a water bottle on the coffee table and handed it to her husband. “Here, drink this,” she said.

He let her put the bottle to his lips, and he took small snips. I wondered when he last ate.

After he drank, Madeline helped him sit in a rather comfy looking club chair, and she motioned for me to sit beside him in the second chair.

The room was a little warm and dark with the sliding door closed and covered with blinds. The furniture was older but serviceable and rather comfortable. I watched George as he shook.

“Can you tell me what happened?”

“I…” he cleared his throat again and took a breath. “When Marvin was killed, I panicked. I prepared to leave. I knew I was next.”

He fiddled with his hands and didn’t look at me.

“Everything was falling apart. Marvin was killed to teach Janelle a lesson. They knew she wanted out and must have found out about the FBI. I was next, so I left.”

“You faked your own death and sent the pictures to Madeline,” I said.

George nodded. “I thought if they believed I died, they’d leave Maddie alone. But then Janelle. They killed Janelle!” he shouted with his shaky voice.

"They didn't kill her. Her ex-boyfriend killed her," I said. "He was arrested last night. He's in jail."

"Sebastian didn't kill her?" He finally looked at me.

"Sebastian didn't kill her."

"Neal killed her? Why?" He appeared genuinely confused. "He loved her."

"She didn't love him. He couldn't take the way she treated him."

George nodded as if he understood that.

"Katrina posted bail the first time he was arrested and kidnapped him. She escaped and Neal went back to jail."

George sighed heavily. "Katrina and Sebastian. Have they found them?"

"No. So why am I here?" I asked Madeline.

"He needs help. A doctor. Do you know someone who's discreet?" Madeline asked.

I didn't know that someone. I texted Stan though.

Really? he asked.

Yes.

I'll be there soon.

"He's coming, and we'll get this taken care of," I said without telling them who was coming, though Stan might bring someone else. I couldn't know for sure. And I wouldn't know until after it was almost over.

***

Madeline paced and wringed her hands as George sat slumped in the chair. His eyes were unfocused, and his hands trembled in his lap. I glanced at my phone. It was twenty minutes since I texted Stan.

He could be driving, picking up a doctor friend, or bringing the police. Thoughts rolled through my mind as we waited for help to come.

I heard something outside and peered through the blinds overlooking the backyard. Beyond the backyard was a line of trees that bordered a small forest preserve. I didn't see anything or anyone at the tree line or in the yard.

"What's out there?" Madeline asked.

"I don't see anything," I said.

But then, I heard something close to the house. From inside the locked door, I glanced toward the edge of the back wall, but there was no one there. I walked up the stairs to the main floor and glanced outside the front door.

Katrina leered at me; a gun pointed right at me. I ran for the living area, away from the bullet she shot from the gun. My heart pounded. I felt nauseated as she broke out the rest of the glass from the window on the door and let herself in.

"Nikki Page, how nice to see you again."

I was cowering on the floor beside the chair. "I'm not here to kill you, Nikki. I'm here for George. He screwed up and needs to be punished," she said as she smiled.

"The police are coming," I said. I wasn't sure if that was true, but someone was coming.

"Aw. That's cute. I'm not worried about a few police. Where is he?"

I shrugged. She pointed the gun at my head.

"Really? Where do you think he is?" I said.

I looked at the stairs. Lying to her would benefit no one, and I needed to get out of here alive.

"Get up," Katrina said, again, waving the gun in my direction.

I stood, my legs trembled as I walked past her and down the short flight of stairs. I glanced at Madeline, and she tensed at the sight of Katrina and the gun.

"Why can't you leave us alone!" Madeline screeched.

"Madeline. Maddy. Listen to me. You knew what you were getting into when you convinced George to join us. You've reaped the rewards for all he's done. Look around." Katrina eyed the small yet well put together house. I knew the area was expensive, even this smaller house. Possibly to hide their misdeeds.

I shouldn't have been surprised that Madeline knew everything.

"You lied to us, you bitch," Madeline shouted. It was a voice and an attitude I had yet to see in her. She always came off as meek and frightened.

"Look who's come off the bench. Tsk, tsk, Maddy." Katrina, again, pointed the gun at Madeline.

"What good is it gonna to do to kill us? The police will know it's you," I said, though my voice shook, and I was sure Katrina knew I was scared.

Katrina craned her neck in my direction, her eyes wild. "No comments from the…" she smiled. I followed her gaze. Sebastian, the face I remembered from the pictures on Janelle's social media smiled a wide smile.

"Hi, love," Sebastian said as if he hadn't walked into a house with three hostages.

"It took you long enough to get here. Tie them up, won't you?" she said in a sickeningly sweet voice.

I hadn't noticed the bag at first, it was black like his jeans and his shirt. He dropped it on the floor, opened it and pulled out rope and a knife.

Sebastian's piercing blue eyes against his black hair gave him an air of sophistication and sexiness. I could see why Janelle was wrapped up in him. But he terrified me. He glanced around the room, and then upstairs.

Without a care, he strode up the stairs and easily lifted two chairs from the kitchen and carried them back down to us. He put them across from each other and looked at me. “Sit,” he said.

I did as he told me to, and as I did, I saw George, still not moving but looking on in terror. I wish he would do something, but he seemed paralyzed by what was happening.

Sebastian grabbed the rope and began tying my hands behind me. I held my breath when he yanked on me again. I could feel it in my shoulders as I let out a yelp, I hadn’t meant to let out.

“Princess. Be good, and you’ll get out of here just fine,” he said.

I didn’t believe him.

***

I thought of the kids, of Will and the mess this case had become. I was stuck in here with a mad man and a mad woman and even as my brain ran through the possible scenarios, I couldn’t fathom how I’d get out.

When Sebastian pulled on the rope one more time, he decided I was secure enough and stood again.

“You next, lovely lady,” he said to Madeline.

She shook her head in fear. “Why are you doing this? Don’t you know she’s setting you up!” Madeline was shouting, her voice trembling.

“Oh Maddy, come on. You know what’s going on.” He pointed the knife in George’s direction. “George screwed up.

Janelle got killed because he wasn't paying attention. We lost our best agent."

It took all I had to breathe as he spoke.

"It wasn't my fault," George said. His voice was still shaky, and he sounded as if he was miles away.

"Why did you kill Marvin?" I asked. I had nothing left to lose. Though knowing wouldn't help anyone if I were dead, and I regretted asking when Katrina glared at me.

Her face softened immediately, and she smiled at me. "Marvin was becoming a problem. He was helping Janelle escape, and we couldn't have that. He had to be taken down a notch." She pointed her chin in Sebastian's direction. "He got a little aggressive with Marvin and well…" She shrugged carelessly.

My mind raced. Marvin didn't have anything on them that Janelle didn't have. Was there more hidden in his house?

"That doesn't make sense. Marvin didn't have any evidence Janelle didn't have. I think she asked him to hold on to copies of what she had. He was helping her, but you wouldn't kill him because he was holding on to evidence you didn't bother to look for. His house was in perfect condition when he was found. So why did you kill him?"

I matched Katrina's gaze.

She laughed. It was the first time I've heard someone laugh an evil laugh.

“Well give the busy body a gold star. You’re not as stupid as you look.”

I didn’t know if I should be proud or offended. I let myself be both.

Katrina, not one to get her hands dirty, grabbed Madeline by the upper arms and pushed her toward the second chair. “We don’t have time for this,” she said through gritted teeth.

“Leave her alone!” George shouted as Katrina pushed Madeline into the chair.

“Tie her down!” Katrina ordered.

George finally stood. Finally moved out of his stupor. He ran at Katrina.

“This is all your fault!” he shouted as he lunged at her. He was heavier than Katrina by at least 100 pounds, but he wasn’t exactly stronger.

George pushed Katrina back. They fought over the gun rocking and pushing each other in an unsteady wrestling match, with the gun waving about.

I worked on the rope that tied my hands back as Sebastian worked to tie Madeline to the other chair.

“Help me, you moron!” Katrina shouted.

Sebastian left the rope untied. Madeline stared at me, fear on her face. I nodded, but I’m not sure what it meant for either of us.

I watched as the rope slipped to the floor, and Madeline rushed to me. She easily released the rope around my ankles.

"Who's coming?" she asked as she cowered behind me.

I couldn't stop the trainwreck of the wrestling match as the gun was still bandied about. Outside, police sirens wailed, growing louder as they got closer. I knew Stan would come through.

Katrina, with her hands on the gun, looked at Sebastian. "Do something about the police!" she shouted as she pushed her thin frame against George.

Cars screeched to a stop outside the house, and the gun went off.

For the longest moment, no one moved.

I saw the blood on the carpet, and then George crumpled to the ground.

Everything else happened so fast.

"George!" Madeline moved toward him.

Katrina aimed her gun at Madeline. "Keep her back. Say anything, and you'll be next."

I held on to Madeline as she trembled in my arms.

Katrina watched us from the top of the short staircase as Sebastian set up beside the front door.

I heard the gun cock.

Voices barked orders and footsteps pounded the cement. Katrina looked around the room for her escape, but the voices were heading around the back of the house toward the sliding door.

"Shit!" she shouted. When a wild animal knew they were in danger, they were willing to risk it all. There were two hostages in the den with her, and we'd be her ticket to freedom. I held Madeline tighter.

"Police!" a voice shouted through a bullhorn. He came from out front.

"You need to let us go, or they're coming in and someone else is going to get hurt," I pleaded as I saw George bleeding out on the floor.

"NO! I need to think," Katrina shouted.

She paced. Voices became more harried. George gurgled out his last breaths. I glanced through the small slit in the blinds. There were five officers in the back yard, guns pointing at the door.

I had to think. I had to let them know where we were, and I needed to get Madeline and myself out of the way. She was still in my arms.

I released one arm from around her shoulders and watched Katrina, still thinking of her next step.

The wall phone rang and today that shocked me. Katrina stopped. Looked at Madeline. "Answer that!"

Madeline went for the phone.

"He…hello," she said as Katrina aimed the gun at her head.

"Mrs. Egan. Is Sebastian and Katrina Winston with you?" a female voice asked.

"Yes," she answered.

Katrina grabbed the phone. "What do you want?" she groused.

"Let them go," the voice said.

"No. I want you to back off. Let me get into my car or the hostages will be dead. It'll be your fault."

She slammed down the phone.

"They're moving closer to the house!" Sebastian said.

"Then shoot!" Katrina yelled and sighed deeply. "Dumbass," she murmured. Sebastian, who I assumed was more competent than this, shot at the police.

The phone rang again. "Katrina, you're only making this worse. Call him off," the voice said.

"I want to be let out. I'll be bringing one of the hostages with me." She slammed down the phone.

It was now or never as I reached for the stick on the blinds. Madeline watched me, and I waved her over. She and I ran past the sliding door, revealing the scene inside. Another gun shot rang out from the front door.

We ducked behind the wall as a bullet pierced the glass and shot into Katrina's shoulder.

She spun and fell down.

Sebastian shot out into the police and when he ran out of bullets, he ran upstairs. The police, seeing Sebastian gone, ran for the front door and busted in while the team out back crashed a battering ram through the back sliding door.

With guns trained on Katrina, she saw her way out. She raised the gun to her forehead and shot herself.

CHAPTER 26

I was trembling in the back of the ambulance after the EMTs assured me I could go. Madeline was in the second ambulance with her late husband crying. I wanted to console her, but the police had their business to do.

Stan joined me.

"I let Will know where you are and that you're okay. He wasn't happy I didn't tell him earlier. He's on his way."

I smiled, but didn't feel like smiling. "Thanks."

"Are you okay?" he asked me.

I shook my head. "I'm not. I watched her kill George. I watched her kill herself."

And now I watched the police manhandle Sebastian from the house. "It was all Katrina. She made me do this. It was all Katrina's fault," he pleaded.

We always assumed he was the leader, that he was scary and dangerous. But my impressions were changed that day when he pleaded with the cops to let him go, as he whined his way inside the cop car. The police officer pushed his head down and pushed a handcuffed Sebastian inside the car.

Will rushed onto the street. He stopped his car quickly and exited, scanned the area, and I waved when he spotted me.

"What will the police do about Dr. Hubble? He seemed to be the real producer of this mess."

"They're picking him up now," Stan said.

"Nikki. Oh damn. I was so worried." Will wrapped his arms around me and kissed my forehead.

"I'm fine. A little shaken," I said.

"When Stan called…" he choked up. I felt tears run down his face.

"I'm sorry I put you through this again. I am. I can't keep doing this."

"Only background checks for you, Mrs. Page," Stan said with a wink.

"I appreciate that. I think that's the speed I'd like."

I stood and leaned against Will. "I'd like to be there when they interview Dr. Hubble," I said.

"Nikki. You've done enough. Why don't we go home. You got Janelle's killer. You uncovered the scheme. Let's go home," Will said.

I watched the police car carrying Sebastian leave the scene. He was still shouting as they drove away. Katrina's body was now taken out of the house and heading toward my ambulance.

We walked toward Will's car and stopped by Detective Clyde. "We found evidence that Dr. Hubble was the leader of the insurance fraud and drug distribution ring. We're looking for him now. Would you like to be there for Sebastian's interview?"

I looked at Will and knew I was done. Regardless of wanting to see the interview I didn't go. "I'm going to go home. I'm tired."

Detective Clyde nodded and headed back to his car.

"I'll go. I'd like to see how it ends," Stan said and climbed into his own car.

Will got me settled in his car, and we left the remaining crime scene to the investigators.

***

I woke up when the car stopped. We weren't home. We were outside the police station. Detective Clyde had just arrived and was walking to the station.

"Why are we here?" I asked.

"You should see how it ends. You did a lot to find Janelle's killer and you deserve to see the finale." He smiled but he seemed as tired and stressed as me.

"I really was fine going home. I'm exhausted."

"I know. You'll sleep when we get home. You can start later tomorrow. I'll work from home. It'll be great."

We walked through the parking lot, not of the police station, rather we were in a federal building that looked like the local FBI office. Will opened the door for me and walked me inside, his arm protectively around my shoulders. Stan saw me walk in. "I thought you were going home."

"A quick stop."

Detective Clyde attempted a smile when he saw me. "The FBI and DEA will be working this one. Can I get you anything?" he asked us.

I nodded. Will asked for coffee. Stan the same.

I couldn't even think about food.

"Do the kids know?" I asked.

"I didn't have the heart to tell them. I texted them to let them know you were on a case. I told them we'd be home late."

"Thanks."

We rode the elevator up to the fifth floor in silence. I leaned against Will as he kept his arms around me.

We were met by an FBI agent.

"Mrs. Page, Mr. Mann, Mr. Marley. I'm Agent Whitely. I hear you've been instrumental in this case and since you've been vouched for by Detective Clyde, Jackson Beale, and

Roland Lester, we're going to let you in on the final act." She handed us visitors' passes.

"Thank you," I said as I stifled a yawn and put the visitor's pass on my shirt.

Stan, Will, and I were led down the hall to a viewing room and asked to sit in the chairs. Agent Whitely set up the television to the interrogation room where we saw Sebastian anxiously waiting in a chair with what I assumed was his lawyer.

"I'll be inside," Detective Clyde said, and he took his leave.

Sebastian looked anxious; he tapped his foot against the floor and his fingers on the table, stopped, then put them in his lap before placing them on the table again.

"We overestimated how dangerous he was. Trap him in a corner and he breaks down," I said.

"He's still dangerous if the gun's in front of 'em," Stan said.

He wasn't wrong.

"Mr. Winston, you're here because you committed insurance fraud, drug trafficking, distribution, and murder," said Lester Roland.

"I didn't do it. It was Katrina," he said. "Katrina's idea."

"How did Katrina meet Dr. Hubble?"

That question confused and surprised Sebastian.

"I don't know what you mean," he said slowly.

"How did Dr. Hubble and Katrina meet? When, where, how?" Lester Roland asked again. "It's really not a difficult question."

"I…I don't know."

"Mr. Cole. Cole was your birth name. Paperwork shows you changed it fifteen years ago when you worked for Dr. Robert Hubble. Helped you change it, did he? You started working for him fifteen years ago. Kept working for him all these years. Correct?"

"I… yes. He was great. He helped me when I was in trouble. He helped me with my career. I owe him for where I am."

It was the first time since I came in contact with Sebastian where he was assertive, more like what I had expected.

"What did he expect for payment, for all of his… help?" Lester Roland asked.

Sebastian was still trembling, and bouncing his knee up and down. "He… he expected loyalty from me. He gave me jobs. He expected them done."

"When did he bring you into the insurance fraud?" Detective Clyde asked.

"He…"

Clyde opened a very thick folder and pulled out several emails. He placed them in front of Sebastian. "Janelle left us these. You ordering Janelle to take on certain clients. These documents here." He pulled out several claim forms, and slid them over. "And these here are the clients and the work that was done for them. It went through billing." He pulled out more documents, and then said, "From there, it went to Dr. Hubble for approval. Am I missing something?"

Sebastian wrung his hands.

"We think Dr. Hubble has been doing this for years. At least fifteen. He took you in, a troubled young man gave you a new life and for payment, you ran the organization. Did what he asked. And you delivered. Did he order you to kill Marvin?"

Sebastian stopped wringing his hands. "I want a deal?"

Detective Clyde smiled at Lester Roland. Roland looked at Sebastian. "That depends on what you give us."

"Dr. Hubble. He was all of it. He gave me the patients to scout out, based on what he thought we could get away with from their conditions. What could be prescribed. We sent them to Murphy's, to Wellness, to several therapy organizations. George was in on it. Not at first. Janelle brought him in."

When he said that, Will tensed beside me. I reached for his hand and squeezed it. "She had a role. She was stuck and tried to make amends," I reminded him.

Still his jaw clenched.

"When did Janelle come into the plan?" Clyde asked.

"Three years ago. I met her at a conference. Dr. Hubble sent me there to go after her. He wanted Murphy's in the scheme. I found out about St. Thomas, and Katrina and I went to recruit her."

"And Janelle recruited George?" Clyde asked.

Sebastian nodded. "That was the purpose of bringing her in. She was smart, beautiful and had the in. He worked with her before. He knew she'd be perfect. Until she ruined it all," he grumbled.

"You mean contacting the FBI and reporting it?" Lester Roland asked.

"Yes. She was also naïve. She could have been rich. She could have had everything, and she threw it away," he spat.

"She was feeling guilty and wanted to make it right. She did the right thing and you decided to what, kill Marvin to teach her a lesson?" Clyde asked.

"We didn't want her to leave. She was going to ruin it all. We had to let her know that we'd keep killing those around her if she didn't drop it with the FBI. Marvin was perfect."

"Who gave the order to kill Marvin?" Clyde asked.

"Dr. Hubble. He wanted to scare Janelle."

"Did you kill Marvin?"

Sebastian didn't say anything.

"You were his go to," Clyde said. "You didn't kill him?"

"I was his go to for everything else. I didn't kill anybody. Ever. That was Katrina's job. She did it. She killed Marvin. She was going to kill Geroge next. She was pissed that he ran, and she was pissed that Janelle was killed. She did everything she could to make sure that didn't happen."

"You know it was Janelle's ex-boyfriend that killed her. Wanted it to look like whoever murdered Marvin killed her too."

Sebastian nodded.

"And back to Dr. Hubble." Lester started. "How did Katrina meet Dr. Hubble?"

"I don't know. I suppose the day she was born. She was his daughter."

***

Sebastian wrote out a very long confession to Marvin's murder, to George's role in the plan, and how it all played out. He even included how Teddi and Martha had very little roles in the whole thing.

He was tucked away in the jail cell to be moved to a more secure facility in the morning, and last I heard; Dr. Hubble had escaped somewhere. Probably to a country without an extradition treaty. Two murders, his daughter's suicide, two jailed parties. So much bloodshed. All for nothing.

I had slept through the night. Or early morning to afternoon. The kids had been quiet, patiently waiting for me to wake up because after we came home, Will told them what had happened.

They were unsurprisingly worried, and when I came downstairs, they rushed me but stopped before reaching for me.

"Are you okay? Will told us what happened?" Emily asked.

"I'm fine. I didn't go there looking for trouble. It just happened. I'm here. I'm good." I hugged each of them.

They'd stay with me for the rest of the weekend.

Four days after working on a whole host of research projects for Stan, Will joined Jack and I as we took Emily to school. We spent the whole day loading and then unloading the van and helping her set up in her new room with her new roommate Susannah. She was excited to start her sophomore year.

After Emily hugged all three of us, we left her to her roommate and their new school year. We were back on the road before dark.

"So, tell me what really happened," Jack asked as we pulled out of the school lot.

"I went to help a murder suspect, and the really bad guys came to the house and held us hostage," I said. I still trembled thinking about it.

"How do you get into these situations?" Jack asked.

I wasn't sure if he was trying to be funny or if he was really worried.

"I don't know. I hadn't tried to do it. It just happened."

"Are you still going for the private investigator's license?" Jack asked.

"I don't know. I can't keep running into trouble. And bringing the kids into it."

"It's a mistake. You really need to rethink it," Jack said.

"Thanks for the vote of confidence. I'll keep at it but I hope I won't have heavy cases like this ever again. I just want to do my job and come home at the end of the day."

"The kids tell me you're getting married in December?" Jack was fishing.

"We are. And you'll be done with alimony. Lucky you."

"Not lucky. I'll give you a buyout. You deserve the money."

I was surprised by that. Legally he didn't have to do that.

"And you and Amber. Is it getting better?"

He took a quick glance at me. "No. It's really not. She's been out a lot. I think she's having an affair."

It didn't make me happy that he was suffering and going through that. "You sure?"

"Unfortunately, I know the signs."

I couldn't say anything to that. I wasn't surprised after all he had gone through since the baby was born.

It was a very long and silent 47-minute ride.

***

Monday morning was a rush of getting lunches, backpacks

and school supplies together. First Julia, and then Jacob left for their first day of school.

I had one school year left with Jacob and then it would be Julia and me. How did that happen?

They were off to school, and I was studying. I had the test in a week even though I was doubting this as a healthy career option. I knew in the end I would walk down the PI path because I was actually really good at it.

Stan emailed more things that I needed to get done for him, more work, and that felt right. I also had freelance work coming in, documents that needed research and writing. I was finding myself busy enough.

When I was done for the day, I grabbed a mug of tea and stood outside watching a mama deer and her baby graze our apple tree. Will came up from behind me, put his arms around me.

He kissed my neck, and I leaned into him.

"They look happy," he said about the deer.

"Yeah. Not a care in the world."

"Are you nervous about the test?"

I shook my head. "I feel good."

I did feel good. I was finally on the right track and all was the way it should be.

The End

www.ingramcontent.com/pod-product-compliance
Lightning Source LLC
Chambersburg PA
CBHW070843260626
47170CB00007B/2484

* 9 7 9 8 9 9 0 6 1 9 4 5 6 *